A WITCH AGAINST THE VAMPIRE

Supernatural Academy - Book 2

SOPHIE CASTLE

Illustrated by
NATASHA SNOW

Edited by
ELIZABETH LANCE

CONTENTS

CHAPTER 1
BETHANY

I stared at my phone from the backseat of our car for the tenth time.

Come on, James, answer me. Let me know you're okay, I thought with a sigh.

I was worried that he was in the midst of some battle with unknown witches while I was stuck on a road trip with Mom and Dad. I couldn't even sneak in practicing magic because we were together twenty-four seven.

Mom and Dad had insisted we take a month long family vacation before I had to return to Dusk Academy. It was mid-July and we'd spent the last two weeks traveling and stopping at every "must see" sight on Mom's list. I was already exhausted and we still had two weeks to go. We'd just left the giant ball of twine in Cawker City, Kansas, and we were now headed to Fayetteville, Arkansas so Mom could have her picture taken with the giant thirty-foot tall dancing hog.

"Isn't this fun, Bethany?" Mom asked for the tenth time, looking over the seat at me.

"Yeah, Mom. Can't think of anything I'd rather be doing." I pasted a smile on my face and silently wished James would text me back. I'd sent him a message earlier that morning, just a quick, *Hey, how are things going?* But he still hadn't answered.

"Look, it says here that the dancing hog was once a magician! He could turn himself into animals, isn't that neat?" Mom read as Dad drove. "Oh, how sad. It says his spell book was destroyed by the LSU tiger, who was actually their town's biggest rival and he got stuck as the hog."

"That is pretty strange, Mom. Do you think it's real? Like maybe the guy was actually a witch and not a magician?"

"Hmmm, I don't know. Maybe so," she said with a smile. "Oh it says someone, a blacksmith, used some kind of gadget and froze the hog into its current position, which made his eyes turn from brown to blue."

I nodded and then looked back down at my phone and it buzzed. Finally James texted back.

No luck yet. Having a good time with your parents? - James

Kind of, we're going to see a dancing hog statue. :P You? -Bethany

Still out with Lindon. The elders have summoned us, have no clue how that will go. - James

I'm sorry. I hope you find something soon. - Bethany

Me too. Miss you. - James

I smiled. *Me too. - Bethany*

After we saw the dancing hog, and Mom took her fill of pictures, we stayed the night in a cheap motel. The next morning we set off to visit the Arkansas Alligator Farm in Hot Springs. The Alligator Farm claimed to be the home of a Merman, which actually turned out to be a half-fish, half-monkey looking creature, but it wasn't living. I got to touch a young gator, the operator held its mouth shut, which I kind of thought was mean, but I suppose necessary if you were going to allow the creature near a bunch of kids to touch and have their picture taken with.

"Hold his tail," the operator of the farm said with a grin.

I did as he asked and my eyes widened as I felt how powerful the one-year old gator's tail was. "It's already pretty strong," I commented as I held the tail.

"Let me get a picture, Bethany," Mom said, holding up her camera.

I rolled my eyes, but pasted a smile on my lips and posed with the gator.

"Oh that is a good one," Dad said with a chuckle.

I just shook my head and thanked the operator before following my parent thru to the gift shop. Mom got an alligator magnet for the fridge to go along with all the other ones she'd collected on this trip. We had dinner at a BBQ place that claimed to be Bill Clinton's favorite restaurant and then we spent the night there in Hot Springs at another cheap hotel, at least this one had a pool and I was able to escape the room with my parents for a while to swim.

I set my towel down on the patio chair and sent a text to James.

Hey, in Arkansas now, got to touch an alligator, LOL Any news yet? - Bethany

I waited a few minutes to see if he'd text me back, but my phone stubbornly stayed silent. With a sigh, I set the phone on my towel and jumped in the pool. I swam laps for about thirty minutes and then checked again, but still there wasn't anything from James.

Okay, headed to bed. Hope you're okay. Miss you. - Bethany

The next day we spent touring the Josephine Tussaud Wax Museum. Josephine was the daughter of the famed Madame Tussaud, we learned when we entered the museum. It was pretty cool. Mom took a ton of pictures of each of us with all the different wax figures. And at the end of the tour, Mom actually convinced Dad to spend the extra dollars so we could check out the escape route gangsters used to use when the building had been a casino and raided by the cops.

I sent James another text after we hopped in the car again to head to Mom's next "must see" sight. *Just went to the coolest place. Wax figures and a gangster's secret escape from a casino. How is the search going? - Bethany*

The next day I sent him another. *Where are you? Are you okay? -Bethany*

However I never received an answer. I sent him numerous more as we traveled, but each one went unanswered and I was really starting to worry that I'd chased him away.

By the time we finally returned home at the end of July, I was exhausted from all the traveling, and sad about not hearing from James. The last thing I wanted to do was wash all my clothes and repack. All I wanted to do was crawl into my bed and hide, but if I did that, I wouldn't be able to go to school where James was going to be. At least I hoped so. I'd missed him so much, but I hadn't heard from him in two weeks. No texts, no calls, nothing. I was worried that he'd decided he didn't want to see me anymore. Or worse that something had happened to him. Like maybe he was attacked by a Formless One while out searching for the coven of witches who had his sire killed.

Somehow, I knew that wasn't the case. Mostly because Jodie or Fira would have let me know if that had happened. So I shook the thought from my head almost as soon as it occurred. I hoped there was a reason he was avoiding my texts and not that it was because he was no longer interested in me. On top of missing James, I was worried about this school year. I knew I wouldn't be rooming with Jodie again, that I'd have to go back to the witch dorms.

"Bethany!" Mom called from downstairs.

"Yeah, Mom?"

"The dryer's ready!"

Sighing, I trudged down the stairs to get the rest of my clothes.

✦

"I'm so glad we took the summer to travel and get out of the house." Mom smiled at me over the seat.

Thinking back over all the things we'd done in July, I smiled. "It was fun," I agreed.

"Should we plan something for next year? Oh, maybe we could take a cruise, what do you think, dear?" Mom looked over at Dad, trying to draw him into the conversation.

Dad cut his eyes at her and frowned. "We'll see."

"Maybe we could just go to a beach?" I suggested hopefully.

"Maybe," Mom said with a nod. She looked at me again and frowned. "Bethany, there is something your dad and I—" she started to say.

Dad cut her off. "Not now, dear." Dad frowned at her, and gave her a glare that told her he wasn't happy with her bringing up whatever it was she wanted to discuss.

"But—"

"Not *now*."

Mom sighed and I wondered what they were silently discussing between them with their glares and frowns. If I hadn't known better, I would have thought they'd both developed mental telepathy like Luci. Thinking of her, and the others, I became a bit more excited to get back to school.

For the rest of the ride we rode in uncomfortable silence. When we arrive at the town outside of Dusk Academy I was so ready to get out of the car because the tension between Mom and Dad was off the charts.

"Go ahead, dear, we'll be right behind you."

I got out of the car and headed into the crowded

bistro. Looking around there weren't many tables available and it looked as though there was a line of people waiting to be seated. Mom and Dad came in moments later, Mom was smiling while Dad seemed to look defeated.

"Did you put our name in for a table?" Mom asked.

"No, I didn't know where you wanted to sit."

"There's plenty of outdoor seating and it's not too hot, I'll see if we can sit out there." Mom moved over to speak to the hostess and she returned a few minutes later, all smiles.

The hostess followed her with three menus and said, "This way."

We followed her out and she seated us at a table in the middle of the courtyard of the only nice bistro restaurant in the town near Dusk Academy. As we sat, she said, "Your waiter will be with you in a moment."

I watched her hurry back to her station, only to reappear moments later with another couple. Sighing, I picked up my menu and glanced at it. Everything looked good and I was starving.

"Hello again, may I get your drink order? Your waiter will be here in a moment, but we are just a bit busy today," the hostess said with a smile.

"Sure, I'll have a tea," I answered.

"We'll have water with lemon," Mom answered for both her and Dad.

Dad frowned at her, but didn't argue.

"I'll have those out to you in a moment." She left and I went back to my menu.

Before I even had a chance to look past the first page, a glass was set on the table in front of me. I looked up at the waiter as he set down Mom and Dad's drinks.

"Good afternoon. Sorry for the delay, may I take your order?" he asked.

I continued looking over the menu undecided.

"Sweetheart, what would you like to order?" my mother asked.

The waiter, whose name was Devon, hovered over our table. I glanced up at him again and then back to the menu.

"I don't know. Dad, what are you having?" I questioned, hoping for more time. I was torn between the French dip and the turkey club. Both sounded delicious, and the images in the menu looked mouth-watering.

"I'll have the hot ham and cheese on rye with fries," my dad told the waiter.

"Miss?"

I bit my lip and tilted my head at the menu again.

"I'll have…" I sighed, I still wasn't sure which meal I wanted. "Um…"

"Sweetheart, we can't sit here all day, you need to decide," my mother urged me to choose while patting my hand firmly.

I glanced at her and frowned. "Ugh. Fine, I'll have the turkey club." I folded the menu and started to hand it to the waiter, but stopped. "No, wait, the French dip…" I frowned again, second guessing myself as I hesitated. "No, the turkey club."

Devon smirked at me. "Are you sure?"

I nodded. "Yes. The turkey club." I needed to learn to trust my first instinct.

My mother smiled and shook her head at me before looking up at Devon. "I'll have the same."

"Alright then. Two turkey clubs for the ladies, and the hot ham and cheese on rye for the gentleman. I'll have those meals right out to you." The waiter folded his pad, slipped the menus under his arm and headed into the building.

I was enjoying the sunny, perfect weather even though we were sitting at the umbrella tables in front of the bistro café. As much as I loved my parents, and as good of a time as I'd had on our month long sight-seeing trip, I was so very ready to get back to school. Being away from the Academy for the summer had driven me crazy. I couldn't really practice my magic, as we were supposed to keep our abilities away from the general public, and my mom and dad didn't really like me practicing in the house and there was no way I could have on our trip. They hadn't given me hardly any alone time. I figured they were afraid I would try to work some magic. It seemed that my magic made them feel weird, or so they said. But it wasn't as if they could actually *see* me doing it when I did manage to sneak in some practice. I felt so far behind since I hadn't known I even had powers until the summer before. I'd spent the last year trying to play catch up and without much practice over the summer, I feared I'd fallen even further behind.

However, working magic wasn't the only reason I was looking forward to going back to Dusk Academy. No, I was really looking forward to going back because of James. I just hoped he'd want to see me. We'd kept in touch via the phone for the first part of summer, but it wasn't the same as seeing him, and then he'd been so silent for the last three weeks. I worried that maybe he'd found someone else. I hoped that wasn't the case, or that he was laying injured somewhere. I knew he'd been busy with Lindon, searching for that coven, but still.

Just the thought of James made me smile and my heart swell. I thought I'd try once more, send him a text letting him know I was close to the school.

Hey, I can't wait to see you! I'm almost back, having lunch with the parents and then on to the Academy. See you soon I hope! -Bethany

I sighed happily at the image my mind conjured of him, but still no answer came back from him. "I can't wait to see James," I murmured softly as we waited for our food.

"Sweetheart, what do you actually know about this boy?" Mom asked, sounding hesitant and unsure, a worried look upon her face. "I mean other than..." she lowered her voice, "that he's a vampire." She shivered as if a ghoul had just crawled up her spine and it made me mad.

James was a great guy. He was kind and sweet, there was no reason for her to be so icked out by him. "I know lots of things about him, Mom."

"Still, he's a... one of those... *creatures.* Can't you find a nice normal boy to date?" My mother frowned and then she looked around at the other patrons of the bistro, her eyes landing on our waiter. "What about Devon?"

I raised my eyebrows at her and then followed her gaze at the lanky twenty-something year old man who'd taken our orders. "Devon? Our waiter? You want me to date our waiter?" I looked at her as if she were completely insane and rolled my eyes at her in disgust.

"Well, he seems nice, and more importantly, human." Mom pursed her lips and gave me a judgmental look.

"And he's like twenty-seven, Mom. And so not my type." I hissed at her, keeping my voice low. I looked up and stopped talking as the man in question approached our table with our food. Only my appetite was suddenly gone.

"Here we are, two turkey clubs and a hot ham and cheese on rye," he said setting each down in front of us. "Is there anything else I can get for you?"

My mother smiled at him and placed her hand on his arm, and I knew what was coming. I slid down in my chair, completely embarrassed by her.

"Devon, that is such a nice name, are you from around here?"

Devon looked around our table and smiled. "I am, I grew up right down the road. Why do you ask?"

"Oh, well, Bethany here is enrolled at Dusk Academy, and we were curious about the area." My mother batted her lashes at him and smiled.

Oh God, just take me now. I glanced up at him through my lashes and felt my cheeks flame.

"Dusk Academy," he looked at me funny and I noticed he suddenly looked a bit uncomfortable, "ah, well, enjoy your lunch." He backed away from the table.

I smirked, feeling a bit better and picked up my sandwich, glad that he'd high-tailed it away from us.

"Bethany what did you do?"

I glanced over at my mother and frowned with the sandwich halfway to my lips. "Me? I didn't do anything. You are the one who brought up the school," I accused.

"Why did he react that way?"

I rolled my eyes. "Gee, Mom. I don't know. Maybe because it's an academy for witches and vampires?" *Duh.*

My mother frowned harder and I knew she was about to over react. "He shouldn't know that, though. I mean it is supposed to be kept quiet, right?"

I shrugged and shook my head. "Maybe he heard a rumor. Maybe he believes what they actually tell the general public, that it's a private boarding school for unmanageable teens. How should I know what he thinks?" I snorted and returned my focus to my sandwich.

"Eat your lunch, dear," my father put in, ending the conversation, thankfully.

Just as I took my first delicious bite of the croissant with turkey, avocado, cheese, lettuce and tomato, I heard a scream. Chewing and swallowing, I looked up and then down the street on high alert. I couldn't see where the scream had come from and so I shrugged again, figuring I was mistaken. I set my mind on ignoring it. It was probably nothing. Right? I mean it could be kids playing games. *But... It didn't sound like a child's scream.*

"What was that?" My mother spun around in her chair, looking for where the sound of the scream had come from.

"I'm sure it was just some kids playing, dear, sit down and enjoy your lunch." Dad's comment mirrored my thoughts, well, part of them anyway. He turned to me as if trying to distract us. "How is it Bethany?" Dad asked, turning to me.

"Good," I answered, but despite my initial thought to ignore it and Dad's attempt at distraction, I kept my eyes on the street, curious now myself as I ate. The scream really hadn't sounded like a kid playing. Now that I thought about it more and replayed it in my head, it had sounded rather like a terrified woman.

"Mine is also," Dad commented, not that I'd asked.

My mother resumed her seat and picked up her sandwich. After a couple of bites, she set it down and wiped her mouth. As she reached for her water glass, she looked at me and taking a deep breath, she said, "Bethany, honey, your father and I are actually concerned about this James boy. I think we would prefer it if you weren't to pursue a relationship with him."

Her words set my heart into a free fall. I set my sandwich down, rattling the plate and looked back up at Mother, feeling quite hurt. I felt tears spring to my eyes as the thought of not seeing James hit me, but I couldn't let her know how much her words bothered me. I had to get her to see that James wasn't dangerous and she was worried for nothing.

All thoughts of the scream vanished. Taking a breath, I said, "There is nothing to be concerned about, Mom. James is a nice boy, there is nothing wrong with him! You are just prejudice against him because he's not like us." I frowned at my parents, my appetite gone once more. I looked down at my sandwich and my stomach felt sick.

"No, sweetheart, it's just... well, okay maybe we are, but that doesn't mean we aren't—"

Another loud scream pierced the air, this time sounding much closer.

My mother whirled in her seat, her glass spilling as she did so. "What was that?" she asked, sounding concerned.

"I'm not sure, maybe I should go—" I started to rise, my heart beating frantically in my chest.

"Oh, no you are not! I will not have you chasing after whatever that is and getting hurt!" My mother gripped my arm. "Tell her to stay here!" she demanded of my dad.

"Honey, I'm sure the police are better equipped to handle whatever that was. Just sit down."

Worried, I resumed my seat, but I still didn't pick up my sandwich. Unlike my parents, I was fairly sure that whatever had caused that scream wasn't something the police could or would handle. I frowned, biting my lip, watching the street again. It was mostly deserted, except for those of us sitting in the tiny fenced in area in front of the bistro café and a couple walking hand in hand toward the bistro. I wanted to warn them, the panic in me building.

"Maybe we should move inside?" my mother suggested as suddenly a short, Asian looking vampire appeared behind the couple. Mother's eyes widened and she screamed as the vampire pulled the woman back by her neck and bit her.

"Great," I muttered, unsure of what to do. The guy didn't look familiar, so I knew he wasn't from the academy. And there was something weird about him. As he got closer, dragging the woman with him as he hopped forward toward all of us behind the low fence, I noticed black webbing crisscrossing over his face and arms along with a blue mold like substance covering his body. He was clearly a Jiangshi vampire and it made me wonder what in the world he was even doing here. He should be on his way back to China, not stealing energy from unsuspecting humans.

"In the café! Now!" my father ordered, jarring me from my thoughts and dragging my mother and me from our seats.

"Dad, no, I have to go help—" I pulled my arm free from him and hurried toward the Jiangshi vampire. *I have to do something!* I couldn't allow him to attack anyone else.

"Bethany!" my dad called from the glass door.

I ignored him, moving forward to place myself between the Jiangshi and the patrons of the bistro café. I studied the creature before me and recalled from the Codex that the Jiangshi were bodies inhabited by their spirit, looking for a way back to their home in China. They attacked humans and supernatural without prejudice, drawing their life force out to keep the body moving in the direction they needed to go, but they couldn't move normally, they tended to 'hop' to where they needed to go.

The Jiangshi dropped the drained woman to the

ground next to the low, white fence between us and fixed its dead eyes on me as it hopped toward me. I drew up my magic, forming a ball of energy and blasted him back several feet. He seemed stunned for a moment, but it didn't seem to affect him for long as he once again began hopping forward.

"Miss Welch!"

I heard my name called and I tilted my head slightly, not taking my actual gaze from the Jiangshi. I couldn't afford to allow him any closer. "Professor Singh!" I called, thankful that she had appeared. "What do I do?"

"Bethany, back away, now!" Professor Singh shouted at me. And then, taking command of the scene and stepping in front of me, she said, "Surround him!"

I did as she suggested, backing up, lowering my hands down to my sides, feeling for chairs and tables in my way as I moved. I scooted around a chair as I watched Professor Singh and the others who'd come with her attempt to move in on the creature. However, the Jiangshi apparently only had eyes for me as he hopped forward blanking out for a moment and then appearing outside of the circle they'd created around him and came right toward me. My eyes widened, as he was not less than a foot away.

"Bethany," my mother whispered urgently in my ear, having come out of the bistro to reach for me.

"Mom, go back insi—" I stated as the Jiangshi hopped right in front of me so quickly it was all I could do to throw some counter magic at him again as I backed quickly into my mother.

The Jiangshi made a weird noise, but continued to push forward again.

"Now, Mom!" I shouted, pushing her with my hand, which I really needed to control my magic, but I couldn't let my mother get closer to the thing. "Please!"

"But—"

Professor Singh was by my side in the next second and she pushed us both back toward the door enough for my father to grab us both and pull us behind the glass door. I watched as Professor Singh and the others with her, moved in again and then a magical band slid down over the Jiangshi encasing it and containing it. I sighed in relief. It wouldn't be able to get away now. Professor Singh was brilliant with wards and she would have warded that magical band with a whole lot of power to keep the Jiangshi from hopping any more.

"I heard that they had a new band of Dusk Knights," someone commented. "Guess that's them."

I looked again at the other people with Professor

Singh and wondered if the commenter was right. Since the Jiangshi was contained, I reopened the door and stepped outside to ask the Professor if there was anything I could do to help.

"Professor?"

Professor Singh wiped her brow and looked up at me. "Bethany, well, you do seem to show up at the most distinct times, don't you?" She smiled at me and it seemed genuine. "Welcome back."

"Thank you, Professor—" I started, but was quickly interrupted by my mother.

"What is that creature and why was he attacking everyone?" my mother huffed.

"Dear, maybe you should calm down?" My father gripped her arms, but she quickly shrugged him off.

"How are we supposed to allow our daughter to go to a school with these—" she waved her hand at the creature, "things and not be concerned about her safety?"

Professor Singh smiled, though I noticed it didn't quite reach her eyes. "Mrs. Welch, I assure you, this particular creature is not an attendee of Dusk Academy. He is in fact not even alive. You see, the Jiangshi are dead creatures who merely wish to have their bodies returned to their home. We will see to it that he is shipped back home and buried properly in China. There is no need for you to worry."

"No need?" my mother shrieked. "What about that poor woman over there on the ground! This thing killed her!"

Professor Singh sighed. "She is not dead, merely unconscious."

I looked at her strangely, as I knew that was a lie. The woman was most certainly dead, but I wouldn't contradict her. Not right now.

"She's not dead?" My mother started to back down.

"Of course not," Professor Singh soothed.

A few of the people she'd arrived with, the Dusk Knights, from what the person in the bistro had said, went over to the woman and gently picked her up, cradling her. They set her in the back seat of a car and then climbed into the front seats.

"You see, my knights are taking her to the hospital now to be checked out. She'll be fine."

As I watched, the knights began passing out cups of tea. I had a feeling they were laced with something to make them all forget what they'd seen and when they approached me, I declined it. "Thank you, no, I'm fine, though my parents could probably use a nice calming cup."

The knight glanced at Professor Singh, who waved her hand, and then he nodded and handed my parents delicate china cups on saucers.

I sighed in relief as both of my parents sipped their cups of tea and sat back down at our table. "Thank you, Professor," I murmured.

"My pleasure, Miss Welch. I will see you soon, I imagine." With a nod, Professor Singh and her knights left the area.

As I waited for the other bistro café patrons to resume their seats, I cleaned up the spilt water from the glass my mother had knocked over earlier. Then I picked up my sandwich and took another bite. I wasn't really hungry, but I pretended as if we hadn't just been interrupted by a dead man searching for his way home by taking lives.

"Where was I?" my mother asked abruptly a minute later. She set her cup in her saucer, the tea completely gone.

I glanced up and decided to bite the bullet. She would recall anyway in a few minutes. I might as well get on with it. "You were explaining why you thought I shouldn't date James."

She gave me a look that said she didn't like my attitude. "Well, I don't."

"Dad?" I looked up at him, hoping he would make her see reason.

"Sweetheart, we just want what is best for you, and we just don't think dating this particular boy is the right choice."

I sighed. "Are you not going to let me return to the Academy if I tell you I'm still going to see him?"

"Bethany, I know you have to associate with... people like him at school, we would just feel more comfortable if you didn't seek this boy out for other attentions..." my mother trailed off, her gaze going to my dad. "We just want you safe."

"I am safe, Mom. I am safer with James than with anyone!" I exclaimed, dropping my sandwich again. I couldn't pretend to eat it anymore. I was tired of it and of them. "Can we go now?" I asked, leaning back in my chair and crossing my arms.

My dad nodded and waved to Devon to bring our check.

"Here you are, sir." Devon appeared, handed the black folder with our bill to my dad and then scurried away, giving me a wide berth.

I smirked and realized he'd seen me using magic and now his thoughts were confirmed. I was a witch. He hadn't drank the tea, obviously.

My dad placed a couple of bills in the black folder and stood. "Let's get you to the school."

I shoved my chair back from the table and stood. I followed them out of the little white gate and to the car. Pulling open the back door, I settled in the back-seat with a sigh. We drove in silence and I had never happier to see the looming main building of Dusk

Academy in all my life. As soon as the car stopped, I pushed the door open and hopped out, pulling my bag behind me.

Setting my bag on the ground, I turned to my parents and pasted on a half a smile. "Well, I guess this is it."

My mom pulled me into a hug. "I love you, Bethany. I just want what's best for you."

I sighed, but nodded, and didn't say anything. I couldn't, it would break my heart.

My mom let me go and then Dad folded me into his arms. "I'll talk to her," he whispered and my heart lifted. "I love you, kiddo, just know that we have your best interests at heart."

"Love you, Daddy," I commented, my throat feeling tight as I backed away.

Picking up my bag, I gave them a wave and then went up the steps to the school. I didn't turn back to watch them leave, but I heard the car restart and then drive slowly down the drive. I let out the breath I'd been holding. They hadn't flat out forbidden me seeing James, but I supposed I did need to consider their feelings on him. I was still unsure about where we actually stood anyway. Our last phone call had been nearly a month ago. I didn't even know if he still wanted to be with me since all of my texts were still going unanswered.

Straightening my shoulders, I approached the magicked doors and smiled as I remembered the power they held. I ran my fingers over it and then pushed it open, entering the front hall. I was home.

At the end of school the previous year, Professor Ubel had informed me that I would have to move back into the witches' dorm this semester. I was hesitant about that, because I'd greatly enjoyed my time in the vampire dorms and considering how the witches had treated me, I wasn't so sure I was ready to go back. I stood in the great front hall looking around.

"Are you lost, Miss Welch?" Professor Zin asked.

I turned, glancing down to see her approaching me and smiled.

"Surely being away from school for the summer would not make you forget where your dorm is?" She arched a brow at me, her tiny hands on her hips.

My smile grew. "Hello, Professor Zin. No, I am aware where the witch dorms are. I was just... thinking."

Professor Zin nodded, and gave me an encouraging smile. "It will be alright, Bethany. We've placed you with Helen." She reached up and placed a comforting hand on my elbow.

I breathed in, suddenly feeling relieved. While Helen and I'd had our ups and downs over the last year, I still thought she was one of the nicer witches that I had met. Helen was a healer, and a good one. We'd been friends before everything went down with Victoria, and we'd started to get closer again after, but so far it hadn't been the same. Maybe now, after the summer away, things would be better between us. "Thank you, Professor. That is good to know."

"Go on now, classes start in the morning, first thing."

I nodded, picked up my bag and headed toward the witch dorms.

CHAPTER 3
BETHANY

I peeked in the room and taking a deep breath, knocked once on the open door. I smiled, tentatively, when Helen looked up. "Hi."

Helen stood and crossed the room, opening the door wider. "Hi." She looked down, shyly, but it also seemed like she must have felt a little guilty.

I entered the room and set my bag down. Looking around the room, I realized the stuff I'd left in my old room in the vampire dorm had been moved here. The nice bedding I'd acquired, my books, and some of my clothes were already set up for me. "Did you?" I gestured at my bed.

Helen nodded. "Yeah." She looked up at me, hesitantly. "Bethany, I'm so sorry about everything last year."

"It's okay. I do understand, I was hurt, but, I

understood. Victoria was a bully and she threatened everyone."

"I know, but I shouldn't have let that keep me from being your friend." She looked down again, tears spilling on her cheeks.

I moved forward and hugged her. "It is okay, Helen. Really. Don't cry, please. I forgive you. I mean that when it came down to it, you and the others all had my back. Everything worked out." I hugged her tighter and Helen finally wrapped her arms around me.

"I should have insisted you move back over here after it all happened, I shouldn't have left this to now—"

I leaned back and smiled, shaking my head. "I wouldn't have come, I liked being over there. I was comfortable and I have friends there. I wasn't ready to be back over here." I really had felt more comfortable with the vampires than with the witches, even after everything played out. To be honest, I probably would still be over there rooming with Jodie, if Professor Ubel hadn't insisted I move back to the witch dorms. "I know Victoria is gone now, but there are still some who look at me like I was the one who caused everything."

"She was very manipulative," Helen agreed. "They just didn't know if they could trust you. But I do,

Bethany, I promise I do," Helen insisted. She lifted her tearstained face to me and I could see the trust in her eyes.

I smiled and hugged her again. "Thank you." Pulling away, I looked around the room again and then picked my bag up and carried it over to my bed.

"Want some help unpacking?" Helen asked timidly.

Nodding, I said, "Sure."

Together we made quick work of getting the rest of my clothes put away in the small dresser and hung in the closet, as well as getting all my toiletries stowed away. Once we'd finished, we sat down on our own beds. It had been a long day already and I yawned. Traveling a few hours in the car and then the events of the afternoon were catching up on me.

"Are you tired?" Helen asked seeing my yawn.

I nodded giving her a rueful smile. "Yeah, it's been an eventful afternoon. Not only the drive, but then there was a Jiangshi that attacked in town when I was having lunch with my parents. Luckily, Professor Singh and the Dusk Knights showed up and were able to contain him. But I did have to use some magic and it's left me feeling a bit tired."

"Oh my gosh! Seriously?" Helen's eyes widened. "What did it look like? I've never seen one except in textbooks."

"It was kind of weird," I said thinking back over what I'd seen. "I mean, aside from the blue mold and the rigor mortis, he had this weird black webbing all over him."

"Ewww." Helen squished up her nose at my description. "So you saw the Dusk Knights?"

"Yeah, about ten of them, including Professor Singh," I acknowledged. "I had no idea we had so many here."

"There are quite a few here, like about fifty actually." Helen leaned toward me and whispered as though she feared being overheard. "They've built another building toward the back of the school property to house them all. I think they stayed here over the summer, in the witch and vampire dorms." She shivered. "They're kind of creepy, don't you think?"

I frowned, I hadn't seen anything creepy about them. "What do you mean?"

Helen leaned in again and whispered, "They are always so silent and they march around the campus like some kind of military drill team. It's just weird and kind of creepy."

I grinned. "Well, they were effective in capturing the Jiangshi and they passed out this tea that made all the normal people forget what they'd seen, so I guess that's kind of creepy, but I suppose they had to do it.

It's not like we can have them remembering something like that." I shrugged my shoulders.

"True." Helen sighed.

I smiled. "So how was your summer?" I asked, curious to hear about what she might have been up to.

"It was good," Helen said with a grin. "I got to work with my coven, visiting hospices and helping to heal some sick witches. I learned a lot." She looked more confident about her abilities than she had the year before. "How about you? Did you do anything exciting?"

"Well, nothing like that. I hardly got to practice my magic at all. Mom and Dad are kind of weirded out by it." I shrugged. "We did take a family vacation, traveling all over the mid-west, seeing all these bizarre things. It was kind of fun. Mom took a zillion pictures." I laughed.

"That sounds fun, sorry you didn't get to practice much though."

I nodded, nervously picking at a piece of nonexistent lint on my jeans. "So... have you... have you seen James around?" I asked, biting my lip, half afraid of what Helen had to say, and half excited. I really had missed him dreadfully, but I had no idea what he'd done or how he'd spent the last part of his summer since I hadn't heard from him since mid-July. I was terrified that I had turned our relationship into something more than it was. That I would see him, and he would treat me as if we were just friends and not something more.

Helen looked up at me thoughtfully, and said, "Well—"

CHAPTER 4
JAMES

I trudged up the steps to Dusk Academy. It had been a very long summer, following Lindon and the elders of the clan around, trying to discover more information about the corrupt witches and if they were using the Formless Ones to do their bidding. The clan elders hadn't been interested in the battle Cory and I, and the rest of the Academy had waged on Victoria and the Formless One who had appeared and attempted to take down the school. Their only focus was finding out how the coven had managed to get a Formless One to possess a vampire. And not just any vampire, but a master.

The last two weeks of July and the first week of August had been spent at the council speaking with the elders about what Lindon and I had been doing to discover the coven. Most of the elders weren't interested in what was going on at Dusk Academy, as they felt it would surely fail because the witches were evil. That wasn't how I felt, nor was it how Cory and my other classmates felt. We had been part of a successful mission with the witches and had even managed to make friends with a lot of them. Like me, some of them were even dating a witch.

One of the main reasons I was so happy to be back at the academy was Bethany. She was the reason for the smile on my face, despite everything that had occurred. I couldn't wait to see her. The summer without her had been torture. I had texted with her for most of the summer, but when we got to the council my phone wouldn't pick up a signal. I kept getting the out of range message, which had been extremely frustrating. When I returned to civilization, my phone was filled with texts from her that told me she was worried, and I wanted to go straight to her and assure her that I was fine, that we were more than fine. However, before I could go to her, I had to return to my dorm room and get unpacked.

My best friend, and roommate, Cory had managed to return a day earlier, since, unlike me, *he* hadn't been dragged out on another useless quest with Lindon to find out more information, which had turned into a yet another dead end, or before the elders to describe what kind of fruitless efforts had been made to find Arrond's killers. I hoped Cory had seen Bethany and knew where I'd find her.

"Hey Cory," I said as I entered our room, setting my bag down at the end of my bed.

"Hey man," Cory replied, looking up from his comic book as he lounged on the bed. "I see Lindon finally gave you a break." He chuckled.

I rolled my eyes. "You know, I love the guy like a father, but come on." I dropped on my bed. "It's like we're beating a dead horse. I know how Arrond was killed, and that we're searching for information on the coven behind it, but everywhere we turn, it's another wild goose chase with no end in sight. And the elders. Don't even get me started. It just gets tiring." I wiped a hand over my face and then scruffed my hair.

"Better you than me." Cory grinned and tossed the comic down, sitting up. "So, did you hear the news yet?"

I arched a brow at him. "What news? I basically just got here, man. Didn't stop to chat anyone up, just came straight here." Leaning over, I opened my suitcase and began shifting piles of clothes into the dresser closest to my bed.

"Bethany tangled with a Chinese Hopper."

I squeezed the toothpaste tube I'd just grabbed and the toothpaste squirted out all over the place.

"What?" Fear rolled through me and I looked at him with panicked eyes.

Cory chuckled. "She's fine, man, chill. Professor Singh and those Dusk Knights took care of it, but seems she and her parents were at the bistro in town, seated outside, so they got a front row seat to the action. Bethany apparently tried to fight the Jiangshi, but the professor showed up and they took care of it, binding it and stuff. Guess they are gonna send him home." Cory shrugged and picked up his comic again, reopening it.

I felt as if the air had been sucked from my lungs. The thought of Bethany fighting a Jiangshi on her own terrified me. Not that she couldn't handle it, just the fact that she'd had to. She shouldn't have to do things like that. Protect everyone. It was too much to lay on her beautiful shoulders. I needed to see her. *Right now,* I thought and then looked at my hands and shirt. I'd need to clean up the toothpaste first.

I rushed down the hall into the bathroom, leaving my things half unpacked. I quickly took care of the minty toothpaste on my hands and tossed the now useless tube in the garbage. I'd get another later. Once my hands were clean, I practically ran from the bathroom, down the hall and pulled open our dorm room door. I pulled off my shirt and flung it on the floor. Grabbing another from the suitcase, I dragged it over my head and rushed out the door. Before I got too far, I paused. Shoving my head back inside the dorm room, I said, "I'm going to see Bethany."

"Figured you would." Cory laughed and turned a page on his comic.

I stormed through the halls barely acknowledging those who were in my way. It was as if I had blinders on, I couldn't see anything but the path I needed to travel to get to Bethany.

"Hey!" Jodie called as I practically shoved her out of the way. "Glad to see you too, James!"

"Sorry, Jodie!" I called over my shoulder. "Have to go see Bethany!" I continued down the hall.

"I've heard she's fine!" Jodie hollered back at me. "Tell her hi from me!"

I didn't bother to reply, instead I took a left and raced up some stairs and out to the courtyard where I decided to shift and fly to her, as it would be faster. I had to see for myself that she was completely unharmed.

CHAPTER 5

BETHANY

"So you haven't seen him?" I sighed, feeling deflated.

"Nope, sorry. Terrance said to tell you Jodie says hi, though." Helen smiled as a tapping noise sounded at our window.

I reached over and moved the curtain. I smiled as I saw the cutest reddish brown screech owl tapping his beak at the glass. "James." Seeing him left me feeling relieved as I opened the window.

"That's James?" Helen asked giggling.

I nodded as the owl flew in and landed on my bed. He then hopped over to rub his feathered cheek against my jean clad leg. "Yes, it is," my smile grew and I ran a finger over his soft feathers, "and he shouldn't be here."

"Why not?" Helen shrugged. "In this form, I'm

sure nobody will even notice." She grinned as she gestured at him. She rose from her bed and closed our dorm room door. "Better safe than sorry, though."

I nodded. "Yeah." Suddenly feeling an overwhelming sadness, my eyes begin to tear up as I knew my parents didn't want me being with him. I had no idea how I was going to tell him. Did I have to tell him? Did he actually want to be with me? Or was he just here in this form to let me down easy? I sighed and brushed a stray tear from my cheek.

"What's the matter?" Helen asked.

I wiped away another tear. "My parents. They think James is dangerous," I said softly as I continued to stroke the owl's head.

"James?" Helen looked at me incredulous. "He would never hurt you. I've seen the way he looks at you. Even in this form, he clearly adores you."

I nodded, my lips quirked up in a half smile. Helen was right. My parents, I knew, meant well, but they didn't understand. How could they? They weren't witches or magical in any way. As much as I knew they wouldn't like it, I wasn't going to give him up. My heart wouldn't let me. "I adore him too." I smiled, blinking away the tears, determined to get rid of my sad feelings.

"How about I give you two some privacy?" Helen smiled. "I'll just go to the common room and see if anyone else has arrived." She stood up and headed toward the door. "Bye James." She waved at the owl as she closed the door behind her.

The owl hopped off the bed and then transformed into James who suddenly enveloped me in a hug. "Are you alright? Cory told me about the Jiangshi." He pulled away from me and looked me over from top to bottom. Spinning me from left to right as he inspected every inch that was visible.

Giggling, I replied, "I'm fine. It was kind of scary, but Professor Singh and the Dusk Knights arrived right in time."

"Are you sure?" James questioned again, clearly wanting to make sure I hadn't even received a scratch. "Jiangshi can be dangerous, there is no reasoning with them."

I nodded. "I know. Their eyes are completely dead. It was clear it was just taking to keep moving forward. I wish I'd been able to stop him killing that woman, and probably there were others in town who it killed too, but that woman..." I shook my head. I felt bad for her, her life cut short way too soon.

"I'm just glad you are safe." He hugged me again. "We consider Jiangshi to be rather tragic, but deadly to anyone in their way. I can't even imagine how you managed to keep him at bay." James shuddered and pulled me close again, breathing in my scent as he squeezed me to his chest.

I smiled, wrapping my arms around him. "Well, I did knock him out for a minute or two, it was enough to allow Professor Singh to get there and help."

"I'm thankful to her." James shivered again and pulled me even closer, though I hadn't thought there was much room between us, he just held me as if he'd never let me go. After a moment, he sighed and slowly released me. He looked at my face, his eyes going tender as he asked, "Now, what had you teary when I arrived?" He slid his hands down my arms and took my hands.

We sat down together on my bed. I smiled, but I knew it didn't reach my eyes.

"Come on, out with it. I caught some of it. Your parents were giving you a hard time about me?"

With a sigh, I nodded. "Yeah. They are worried that you are a vampire. They don't understand. They aren't magical like we are." I frowned, squeezing his fingers in my hand. "They don't understand me most of the time. Sometimes I wish I could go back. Back before that night, before the storm, before I got my magic." I looked up at him, my eyes blurry with tears. "But if I did, it would mean I'd never have met you, and that is something I—" I swallowed hard, looking at him, my hand going to his cheek. "I missed you,

James. So much." My chest was tight and I knew at any moment I could burst into tears, but taking a breath, I leaned into him, pressing my forehead to his and just breathed, trying to keep them at bay.

James smiled. "I missed you too." He wrapped his arms around me and his lips descended on mine.

I felt my toes curl as I slid my hands around his neck and into his hair. My whole body tingled as he held me tight and kissed me, our tongues tangled in passionate battle. When we pulled apart, I was no longer teary and we were both breathing heavy and smiling.

After a moment, when I could breathe easier, I asked, "So, how was the rest of your summer? Did you find anything out about Arrond?"

James shook his head. "Nothing but dead ends. Lindon dragged me all over the country. He's sure he'll find them. It's just going to take time, I guess." He shrugged. "He's so angry and focused on the witches and I... I can't help but think that... that could be me," he said softly. He squeezed my hands in his again. "When Arrond was murdered, I wanted nothing but revenge. Now... now I know not all witches are evil and after power." He gave me a half smile, showing off his dimple. "Some are beautiful souls who want nothing more than to get along and just live their lives."

I smiled at him shyly and leaned in for another kiss. "And I know not all vampires are out to destroy all witches as some of my kind feel. Some vampires are handsome and loving and never harm anyone who doesn't deserve it."

James chuckled. "Speaking of other vampires, Jodie says hi."

I grinned. "How is she? Helen said she and Terrance are still together."

"I expect she's fine, do you want to see her?"

"Oh, can I? Do you think they'd mind invading the dorms again?" I laughed.

"I think they'd be pretty pissed off if you didn't." James laughed with me. "Come on, we've got time before dinner."

CHAPTER 6

JAMES

I tapped my beak at the glass of Bethany's window. I knew it was the right one, because I could scent her anywhere. I noticed the curtain move and then saw Bethany smile as she opened the window.

"That's James?" Helen asked giggling.

Bethany nodded as I flew in and landed on her bed. I hopped over to rub my feathered cheek against her jean clad leg, happy to see her. I couldn't see any damage to her from the Chinese Hopper, but I wanted to shift and ask her about it.

"Yes, it is," she smiled and ran a finger over my soft feathers, "and he shouldn't be here."

I preened under her touch, not really catching the meaning of her words.

"Why not?" Helen shrugged. "In this form, I'm sure nobody will even notice."

She grinned as she gestured at me and I raised my wing at her. She rose from her bed and I watched her close their dorm room door.

"Better safe than sorry, though."

I blinked my eyes and nodded my owl head, grateful to her.

Bethany nodded. "Yeah."

I caught the slight catch in her voice and glanced up into her face, seeing her eyes becoming watery. I fluttered my wings, wishing I could just shift, but I didn't want to do it in front of Helen.

"What's the matter?" Helen asked.

Bethany wiped away a tear. "My parents. They think James is dangerous," she said softly as she stroked my head.

Me? I thought. I made a snuffling sound, attempting to show my indignation at that.

"James?" Helen looked at her incredulous. "He would never hurt you. I've seen the way he looks at you. Even in this form, he clearly adores you."

I blinked gratefully at Helen, but she wasn't paying attention to me, her eyes were on Bethany.

Bethany nodded. "I adore him too." She smiled, blinking away the tears.

"How about I give you two some privacy?" Helen

smiled. "I'll just go to the common room and see if anyone else has arrived." She stood up and headed toward the door. "Bye James." She waved at me as she closed the door behind her.

I lifted my wing at her and as the door closed, I hopped off the bed and then transformed into myself, and then enveloped Bethany in a hug. "Are you alright? Cory told me about the Jiangshi." I pulled away from her, my heart racing as I checked over every inch of her being.

Giggling, Bethany replied, "I'm fine. It was kind of scary, but Professor Singh and the Dusk Knights arrived right in time."

"Are you sure?" I questioned again. I wanted to make sure she hadn't even received a scratch, the Hoppers were extremely dangerous, especially to those of supernatural descent because they offered more power. "Jiangshi can be dangerous, there is no reasoning with them."

Bethany nodded. "I know. Their eyes are completely dead. It was clear it was just taking to keep moving forward. I wish I'd been able to stop him killing that woman, and probably there were others in town who it killed too, but that woman..." Bethany shook her head.

I could see that the event had clearly wounded her soul. She had such a kind heart, and any death, affected her. "I'm just glad you are safe." I ran my hands down her arms. "We consider Jiangshi to be rather tragic, but deadly to anyone in their way. I can't even imagine how you managed to keep him at bay." I pulled her close again and breathed in her scent. She smelled of strawberries and cream and it made me smile.

Bethany smiled. "Well, I did knock him out for a minute or two, it was enough to allow Professor Singh to get there and help."

"I'm thankful to her." I shivered at the thought of losing her, and pulled her even closer, just holding her. After a moment, I asked the other question that had been bugging me since I'd flown in her window. "Now, what had you teary when I arrived?" I took her hand and we sat down together on her bed.

Bethany smiled, but it didn't reach her eyes and I knew she was worried about sharing.

"Come on, out with it. I caught some of it. Your parents were giving you a hard time about me?"

Bethany nodded. "Yeah. They are worried that you are a vampire. They don't understand. They aren't magical like we are." Bethany frowned, squeezing my fingers in her hand. "They don't understand me most of the time. Sometimes I wish I could go back. Back before that night, before the storm, before I got my magic." She looked up at me, her eyes blurry with tears. "But if I did, it would mean I'd never have met you, and that is something I—" She swallowed hard, looking at me, her hand going to my cheek. "I missed you, James. So much." She leaned into me, pressing her forehead to mine.

I smiled, happy that I affected her as much as she affected me. "I missed you too." I wrapped my arms around her and kissed her.

I felt my heart race as she slid her hands around my neck and into my hair. My whole being felt alive at her touch as I held her tight and kissed her. When we pulled apart, we were both breathing heavy and smiling.

After a moment, Bethany asked, "So, what happened? Did you find anything out about Arrond? And why didn't you answer any of my texts?"

"Sorry about that, my phone couldn't get service for about three weeks while we were with the elders. Believe me, I wanted to text you. I did read everything you sent. I'm glad you kept texting and didn't give up on me."

Bethany smiled and kissed me. "So, what about Arrond? Have you and Lindon found the coven yet?"

Feeling an overwhelming sadness at the mention of Arrond, I shook my head. "Nothing but dead ends. Lindon dragged me all over the country. He's sure he'll find them. It's just going to take time, I guess." I shrugged, trying to put the feelings out of my head and approach the subject as if it didn't affect me as much as it did. "He's so angry and focused on the witches and I..." I paused, realizing that I'd been that way at one time, before Bethany. "I can't help but think that... that could be me," I said softly. I squeezed her hands in mine again, so thankful to have her in my life and wanting her to understand. "When Arrond was murdered, I wanted nothing but revenge. Now... now I know not all witches are evil and after power." I gave her a half smile. "Some are beautiful souls who want nothing more than to get along and just live their lives."

Bethany smiled at me shyly and leaned in for another kiss. "And I know not all vampires are out to destroy all witches as some of my kind feel. Some vampires are handsome and loving and never harm anyone who doesn't deserve it."

I chuckled. "Speaking of other vampires, Jodie says hi."

Bethany grinned. "How is she? Helen said she and Terrance are still together."

"I expect she's fine, do you want to see her?"

"Oh, can I? Do you think they'd mind me invading the dorms again?" She laughed.

"I think they'd be pretty pissed off if you didn't." I

laughed with her. "Come on, we've got time before dinner."

"Now?" She bit her lip. "Are you sure it will be okay?"

"I know it will. She wasn't the only one who mentioned you, they all want to see you." I took her hand and led her to the dorm door.

"Okay."

We left her room and traversed the halls of Dusk Academy, making our way across to the entrance to the vampire dorms. As soon as we entered, we were greeted by several of the girls who Bethany had made friends with last semester.

"Bethany!" Jodie greeted and rushed in for a hug. "Girl, I've missed you!"

"Me too," Bethany said softly, her cheeks turning pink at the attention, but she grinned widely at them.

"Tell us everything." Jodie grabbed her hands and pulled her across the room to sit with her and the others.

She looked back at me and smiled as she was tugged down on the sofa into the middle of all the girls. I laughed and shook my head. I started to head over to her, but Cory stopped me with a hand on my shoulder.

"Man, let her have this moment with them. You

can go all protective boyfriend on her later," Cory joked.

I sighed. "I just got her back. I wasn't ready to give her up to the girls completely yet."

Cory laughed. "You shouldn't have brought her over here then, should you have, man?"

I rolled my eyes and laughed along with him. "You're right. I just knew she was missing them too."

"So let her hang for a bit. Come play darts with Kale, Tran and me."

I nodded and followed Cory across the room to the dart board.

"Hey, James. Play teams?" Tran asked, holding up the darts.

"Sure." I nodded.

We spent the next hour throwing darts, until Bethany finished her conversation with the girls and then joined us. I wrapped my arm around her waist and pulled her close, kissing her.

"Ugh. They are getting mushy," Cory complained dramatically.

"Break it up, you two, we're playing darts here." Tran inserted his hands between us. "Five foot distance."

I laughed. "I think I'm done with darts."

"What? Man, you can't leave me hanging! We're about to win!" Cory put in.

Bethany blushed a pretty pink. "Finish your game," she said softly. "I'll wait till you're done."

I sighed. "Fine," I drew out, but grinned. "Where are my darts?"

Cory handed me the three darts.

Instead of waiting my turn, I let all three fly at the dart board, throwing them together. They hit the board within mere milliseconds of each other. All of them right around the bullseye, one actually hitting it dead center. "There, you happy?" I slid my arm around Bethany's shoulders and grinned.

"What the hell, man!" Tran shook his head. "You been holding back?"

I shrugged and with Bethany under my arm, we left the room to Cory's laughter. "Did you have a good chat with Jodie and the others?"

"I did." Bethany nodded. "We're all caught up and I'm welcome here any time."

I watched her cheeks heat at her words. "You are," I agreed, glad they'd made her so happy.

We headed out the door I'd used earlier, entering the courtyard. As we walked, Bethany snuggled into me and I couldn't remember ever being happier. As we strolled back to the witches' dorm, my ears perked up.

"Do you hear that?" I asked, stopping to listen.

Bethany frowned and concentrated for a moment and then said, "It sounds like... a clock."

"It does, but where is it coming from?" I glanced around in the darkening shadows of the building as the twilight hour approached. I moved closer to the building, but the ticking sound continued in another direction. "So odd."

Bethany shrugged. "Well, if it was here, it's gone now. I mean it's getting fainter and fainter."

Slowly, I nodded. "I guess. Just weird." I shook my head. "Come on, I'd best get you back before you miss dinner."

Bethany smiled, taking my hand. Together we reentered the witches' dorms.

"Tell us everything." Jodie grabbed my hands and pulled me across the room to sit with her Noor, Fira and Lily. We'd all gotten to be great friends last year and I was so happy that they wanted to continue the friendship.

I looked back at James and smiled as I was tugged down on the sofa into the middle of all the girls. James laughed at our antics and started in our direction, I hoped to join us, because I wanted him with me, but Cory stopped him with a hand on his shoulder.

"Man, let her have this moment with them. You can go all protective boyfriend on her later," Cory joked.

James sighed. "I just got her back. I wasn't ready to give her up to the girls completely yet."

Cory laughed at him as we watched their conversation. "You shouldn't have brought her over here then, should you have, man?"

James rolled his eyes and laughed along with Cory. "You're right. I just knew she was missing them too." He gave me another look and smiled at me.

"So let her hang for a bit. Come play darts with Kale, Tran and me."

James headed over to the dart board with Cory and I turned to the girls. "How was your summers?" I asked.

"Boring," Noor replied. "My parents don't like me wearing this stuff." She gestured at the make-up and stylish clothes she wore. "I'm so glad to be back here!"

"I got to see Terrance over the summer, so mine was pretty good," Jodie replied. "We hung out, went to the movies and stuff. He took me to this amusement park that stayed open late, it was a lot of fun."

"You two are so cute together," I gushed. "I'm so glad I introduced you!"

"Me too," Jodie agreed.

"I might have to have you hook me up with someone then," Fira put in. "My summer was boring too. My brothers shot down every idea I had."

"They are overly protective of you," Lily agreed.

"Too protective, by far." She sent a glare over at her brothers.

I glanced over to James and grinned as he focused on the dart board as if he was on the hunt.

"What about you? What did you get up to over the summer? Did you get to see James at all?"

"No, he spent the summer out hunting with Lindon, looking for his sire's killer. We texted a lot and he called a couple times. My mom is a little worried about me dating a vampire, but she's also worried about me being a witch and using magic. I didn't get to practice much over the summer."

"Well that sucks." Jodie frowned.

"Well at least you're back here now and you can see each other." Lily smiled. "Hey, why aren't you staying in our dorms again?"

"Ugh. Professor Ubel insisted that I needed to move back over to the witch dorm. It's okay though. Professor Zin put me in with Helen, so at least I get to room with a friend."

"You'll still come over here and see us though, right?"

I grinned. "Of course, as long as you all are sure you want me here."

"Duh. Of course we do!" Fira laughed. "We've stocked the cabinets and everything for you. Got your favorite snack cakes and everything."

I laughed. "Thanks!"

"Not sure how you eat those, they smell like fake sugar to me." Jodie laughed.

"They are delicious though." I laughed with her.

"If you say so."

"So we totally have to plan a couple girls' nights," Lily put in. "After classes start I'm gonna need one."

"We should do a *Twilight* marathon night," Jodie suggested.

"Oh yeah, I could go for some *Jasper Cullen*," Noor agreed.

"Jasper? Are you kidding, *Edward Cullen* is clearly the best," Fira commented with a laugh.

"But they *sparkle*," Lily complained.

"Everybody has a flaw, Lily," Fira replied.

We all laughed. The rest of the hour flew by and I knew I needed to head back to the witches dorm soon.

"I should probably go. If I don't get some sleep before classes tomorrow, I'll be dragging all day."

"Okay, you want me to walk you back?" Jodie asked.

"Nah, James will, I'm sure." My eyes connected with his across the room.

"Of course." She laughed. "Well, don't be a stranger, okay?"

"I won't," I said with a grin as I stood up from the

couch. "See you all later." I waved to them as I made my way over to James. I stepped into his waiting arms and he pulled me close, kissing me.

"Ugh. They are getting mushy," Cory complained dramatically.

"Break it up, you two, we're playing darts here." Tran inserted his hands between us. "Five foot distance."

James laughed while I hid my blushing cheeks in his chest.

"I think I'm done with darts."

"What? Man, you can't leave me hanging! We're about to win!" Cory put in.

I blushed again. "Finish your game," I said softly. "I'll wait till you're done."

James sighed. "Fine," he said, drawing out the word like an exasperated tween. He grinned at Cory and said, "Where are my darts?"

Cory handed him the three darts with green feathers.

Instead of waiting his turn, he let all three fly at the dart board at the same time. I was shocked to see them all hit the board within mere milliseconds of each other. He was good. All of the darts hit right around the bullseye. One even looked like it actually hit it dead center.

"There, you happy?" James slid his arm back around my shoulders and grinned.

"What the hell, man!" Tran shook his head. "You been holding back?"

James shrugged and with a satisfied grin on his face, we left the room to Cory's laughter.

"Did you have a good chat with Jodie and the others?" he asked, looking down at me with twinkling eyes.

The look made my heart skip a beat. "I did." I nodded. "We're all caught up and I'm welcome here any time."

James watched my face and I couldn't stop the heated blush that crept over my cheeks. "You are," he agreed, sounding happier than he had all summer.

We headed out the door, entering the courtyard. As we walked, I snuggled into him. I loved just being in his arms. He made me feel safe and protected. I couldn't help feeling a bit giddy.

"Do you hear that?" He asked a moment later, stopping to listen.

I frowned and concentrated for a moment and then said, "It sounds like... a clock."

"It does, but where is it coming from?" James glanced around in the darkening shadows of the building as the twilight hour approached. He moved closer to the building, but the ticking sound continued in another direction. "So odd."

I shrugged. "Well, if it was here, it's gone now. I mean it's getting fainter and fainter."

Slowly, James nodded. "I guess. Just weird." He shook his head. "Come on, I'd best get you back before you miss dinner."

I smiled and took his offered hand. Together we reentered the witches' dorms.

THE NEXT MORNING, I WOKE FEELING EXCITED about my first day of classes. I dressed in my favorite jeans and a red, long sleeved tee that I pushed up to my elbows. I headed down to the bathroom and brushed my teeth, and used the facilities. When I finished, I waited for Helen in our room to finish in the bathroom so we could go to breakfast.

Helen came in the door a minute later with a smile. "Ready?"

I grinned and together we walked down to the cafeteria. "Are you excited?"

Helen nodded. "Warding with Professor Singh, after last year, it's gonna be a fun class I think."

"Me too." I grinned as I grabbed a plate with a stack of pancakes and a container of syrup.

Helen picked up a plate of scrambled eggs and fried potatoes and we went to join our friends at a table in the middle of the room. I set my tray down next to Finch and then sat down. Helen took the empty seat next to me.

"So who else has warding first period?" I asked everyone at the table and then cut a bite out of my stack of pancakes.

"I've got it second," Finch replied, shoveling a bite of cereal into his mouth.

"Me too, second period." Quinn sliced his pancakes with a knife into multiple bite sized pieces and the drizzled three containers over all of it.

"I'm in second also," Terrance replied, yawning.

I looked at him and grinned. "Did you get any sleep?" I asked, knowing he'd spent a good amount of time with Jodie the night before.

Terrance shrugged and a grin lit his face. "Isn't that what class is for?" He smirked.

Helen giggled. "What do you have first?"

"History of the Magical World. Boring." He closed his eyes and pretended to snore.

"Oh that is with the new professor, Chalcedony, right?" I asked.

Terrance shrugged. "I guess. Why?"

"I've got it second, with James." I blushed as I said his name.

"Ugh. I wish I shared classes with Jodie. Think they'd let me switch to night classes?" Terrance asked, sounding hopeful.

"Doubt it, Romeo." Finch bumped his shoulder and laughed.

"Argh," Terrance groaned. "Whatever, we'd better go or we're gonna be late."

I shoved the last bite in my mouth and picked up my tray, following the others to dump their trash and then Helen and I hurried back to our room to grab our books. We made it to class with minutes to spare.

When we reached the class, we noticed Luci and Porta also had Warding first period. With a wave, we joined them, taking the seats directly next to them. "Hi," I whispered. "Good summer?"

Definitely, Luci said, her voice entering my head.

I thought you might actually use your voice this year, I commented looking at her with a smile.

I would, but Professor Singh just walked in, and I don't want us getting in trouble on the first day. Luci nodded to the front of the room.

Grinning, I nodded in agreement and turned to listen as Professor Singh brought the class to order.

"All right, all right settle down. I know you've all missed each other over the summer, but we are here to learn, so please, give me your attention!" she said firmly.

Class went well, and I left feeling as if it would be my favorite class of the semester. I split off from Helen who was going to a class on healing magic while I made my way to History of the Magical World. As I rushed through the door, I caught sight of James and hurried to take the open seat next to him. I slid into the seat just as the bell rang and Professor Chalcedony entered the room.

The class contained several of the Strigoi vampires aside from James. I recognized some of them from classes I'd had the year before and I smiled at them, giving them a friendly wave.

"Miss Welch." Professor Chalcedony narrowed his eyes at me. "This is not social hour."

I ducked my head, embarrassed at being singled out when I wasn't the only one talking. I got out my text book and opened it.

ॐ

Weeks passed and it was nearing our second holiday weekend. I'd been looking forward to it, hoping for a break from Professor Chalcedony's crazy fixation on vampires and their desire to destroy all witches. It was absolutely ridiculous and I couldn't figure out how the man managed to gain a job teaching at an academy meant to bring witches and vampires together. It seemed as though he was doing everything he could to get the Strigoi in our class to break the alliance.

Silently I slid into my seat next to James and smiled at him. He grinned back at me as he pulled his text book out and set it on his desk. I did the same and then looked up to see Professor Chalcedony's eyes narrowed upon us.

"If you're quite done flaunting yourself at the Strigoi, Miss Welch, we'll begin class."

I shrank down in my seat, a blush creeping up my neck. He was always such a prick!

"Please take out your textbooks and open to chapter twenty-one. You may begin reading about how the vampires destroyed witch covens."

I blinked up at him and frowned. I'd given chapter twenty-one a cursory glance the night before and it had nothing to do with vampires destroying covens of witches. If I recalled correctly, it was about the Salem Witch Trials. I looked over at James who shook his head and rolled his eyes.

"Mr. Barret. Do you have something to say about chapter twenty-one?" Professor Chalcedony asked, his gaze drilling into James, a look of disgust on his face.

James glanced at him, his face practically blank. "No, Professor." He turned to the correct page and wouldn't glance over at me, even though I knew he could feel my eyes on him.

With a sigh, I began to read and I was correct. The entire chapter was about the Salem Witch Trials. Not a mention of vampires anywhere. When I finished I looked up at the professor, who stood glaring at James and two other vampires seated near him.

"It smells in here." Professor Chalcedony wrinkled his nose moving toward the three vampires. "Like rotten blood." He gave them a look of disgust. "Miss Welch, perhaps you would be more comfortable seated elsewhere? Somewhere less... pungent?" He looked at me, and then he narrowed his eyes on James.

My gaze flicked to James and I noticed the twitch in his cheek, which told me he was seconds away from exploding. "I'm fine, Professor."

Professor Chalcedony glanced back at me and shrugged. "If you say so." He turned and moved back to the front of the room. "Now, who can tell me about the destruction of witches by vampires during the Salem Witch Trials?" He looked around the class, but then his gaze returned to the vampires. "Mr. Barret? Thoughts?" He arched a brow at James. "Do please defend the actions of your... species."

James' eyes blazed and I wished I could pull him

from the room with me and we could just get out of there. I had so looked forward to this class with him and now this new professor was going to ruin it with his bigotry and racism. I frowned and glared at him.

James' cheek twitched, but when he spoke, his words were calm. "As per the textbook, Professor, it was the Puritans who put the witches on trial. Most of the women captured and put on trial were later to be found innocent of being witches. They were mostly normal humans, sir."

"Is that what you read?" Professor Chalcedony arched another brow and looked haughtily down at James. "Perhaps you had best read again, Mr. Barret. In fact, all of you will reread the chapter and write me a report of the abuses of the vampire clans toward the witches of Salem." He peered up at the clock. "One thousand words, due tomorrow. Class dismissed," he said as the bell rang.

James was shaking he was so angry, I could see it as he picked up my books as well as his and strode out of the classroom without waiting for me. I hurried after him, catching up to him about three feet from the classroom door.

"James?" I said gently, laying my hand on his arm. "He's just a stupid racist man. Ignore him."

James took a breath and turned into my arms.

I held him for a moment and then leaned back a little to look at him. "You okay?"

He nodded. "Yeah." He swallowed hard. "I might have to drop that class. I don't know if I can handle—"

I lifted up on my toes and kissed him. "Don't leave me in there alone with him. Please?" I smiled and gave him a pleading look.

James sighed and pressed his forehead to mine. He nodded. "I'll try. Ugh. Stupid assignment."

"I know." I rubbed his arm as we started down the hall. I worried that the two of them wouldn't survive the semester, but maybe with me there, James would be able to handle it. I hoped so at least.

❧

"Miss Welch, a moment?"

I had just come out of math class and turned to see Professor Singh waiting for me. "Hello Professor Singh." I smiled. "Did you need me?"

Professor Singh nodded. "Yes, I had hoped to catch you before you left first period, but you appeared in a great hurry." She smiled.

"I'm sorry. I had to get across the building to my History of the Magical World class. Did you need me for something?" I asked, worried that I was in trouble for something.

"I just need to see you in my office this afternoon, after classes are over, of course."

"Oh. Okay, Professor, I will come right after my last class."

She nodded. "Very good. Well, you may be on your way now, Miss Welch. I wouldn't want you to be late to your next class."

Biting my lip, I hurried off to my potions class, still worrying that I'd done something wrong.

CHAPTER 8

BETHANY

"**A**re you in trouble?" James asked as we walked down the hallway together.

I shrugged my shoulders, biting my lip, which was probably a chapped mess now from me worrying at it all afternoon. "I don't know. I don't know what I could have done." I frowned. "She didn't seem angry with me though."

"Well, that's good. You are probably worrying for nothing," James soothed me, rubbing his hands up and down my arms as we stopped about ten feet from the professor's office. "I'll wait for you right here." He took my books from me and kissed my forehead. "Go on."

I took a breath and walked the rest of the way, as slowly as I could, my gut twisting with fear and antic-

SOPHIE CASTLE

ipation. After one more deep breath, I reached up and knocked on the closed door.

"Enter."

With one last look at James, I turned the knob and entered the office. "Hello, Professor, you wanted to see me?"

Professor Singh smiled. "Yes, do come in, Bethany, close the door behind you please."

I did as she asked, shutting the door as quietly as possible. I turned back to her, my hands folded in front of me as I bit at my lip nervously again.

Looking up at me, Professor Singh frowned. "What's the matter?"

I was suddenly confused. "Um, what do you mean? You asked me here?"

"Oh," she smiled again, "nothing to get worked up over, Bethany, I merely had questions for you about that day in town. You were at the bistro with your parents, I believe?"

Taking a breath, I felt relieved and I smiled. "Oh, that?"

Gesturing at the seats in front of her desk, Professor Singh said, "Please, sit."

I took one of the plush plaid chairs. "What did you need to know?" I asked.

"Humor me, Bethany. Tell me exactly what happened. Start with when you arrived at the bistro. Did you know you were going to stop there?"

I frowned and thought back over our trip. "Well, no, not really. Mom and Dad wanted to stop for lunch. They didn't want to go to any of the fast food places, or the diner, so we ended up at the bistro. The tables inside were all mostly full, so Mom suggested we sit outside."

"I see." Professor Singh's brow furrowed and her lips pursed. "Go on, what happened after you sat down?"

I shrugged my shoulders. "The waiter, ummm, I think his name was Devon, yeah, I'm pretty sure that was his name—"

"Did he give you a surname?" Professor Singh interrupted.

I bit my lip as I tried to remember the waiter. "No, I don't think so, but he said he lived in town. My mother tried to set me up with him, she doesn't like that James is a vampire, so we argued a bit, but oh, first the waiter. Um, he took our order and while he was inside, that is when Mom and I argued." I sighed and shook my head, still irritated with her over it. "Anyway, it was after we had our food that I heard the first scream."

"You heard a scream, but you didn't see where it came from?" Professor Singh's interest piqued.

I shook my head. "No, I couldn't see anything yet at that point. I did look down the street to where I thought it'd come from, but no, I don't recall seeing anything odd right then."

"Go on, then what happened?"

"Well, Mom and I were still arguing. And then I heard another scream and that was when I stood up and noticed the Jiangshi. There was a couple in the street, well, to the side of the street, not actually in it exactly—" I shook my head again, I was getting off track with details, "they were close to the sidewalk, but not on it. The Jiangshi hopped from the side of a building about a block away toward the couple, I wanted to help them, but he was fast. Really fast."

"And he went for the young woman? The one my knights picked up in front of the fence?" she inquired.

"Yes, her. The man she was with, I don't know where he went, but as the Jiangshi attacked, he tore down the street in the opposite direction. The patrons who were seated at the tables around us, started screaming and panicking, hurrying into the bistro. My parents went in also, but I thought I might be able to stop it, so I used some counter-magic. It stunned him for a minute, sent him back-wards, but it didn't last. He came at me again, right as my mother tried to grab me and drag me inside." I blinked at her. "That's when you and the knights showed up."

Professor Singh sighed and leaned back in her chair. A frown marred her face and she looked to be lost in her thoughts.

"Professor?"

"Hmmm?" she murmured.

"How... how did the Jiangshi end up here?" I asked one of the questions that had been bothering me. "I don't mean the U.S., I mean in the town outside of Dusk Academy. I mean, it can't be a coincidence, can it?"

Professor Singh's lips curved up in a slight smile. "You are a smart girl, Bethany. That is indeed the question, isn't it? Unfortunately, I don't think you are going to like the answer to that."

I felt my stomach clench at her words. I took a deep breath and said, "Please, Professor, tell me what you've discovered."

Professor Singh leaned forward and clasped her hands together on her desk, looking at me as if she were trying to decide how much to tell me. She nodded her head as if she'd made a decision. "The Jiangshi, it appears was herded toward the bistro. Toward *you*. It had multiple lacerations on its legs, as well as bite marks. In further examination, it appears the bites were venomous. Whether by a creature or a person, we are not sure, yet. However, it seems that this particular Jiangshi had been on a ship, headed back to China just the day before the attack off the coast of Maine, so for it to appear here..."

"Someone had to bring it here," I breathed out, my words barely a whisper.

Pursing her lips, Professor Singh nodded. "After last year, you are... shall we say *known?* There are those who will wish you harm simple because you exist, Bethany."

I swallowed hard, but nodded. "Am I safe here?"

"I would say you are safer here than anywhere else in the world." Professor Singh gave me a comforting smile. "You have me, and the other professors, as well as the Dusk Knights all to watch out for you."

I nodded.

"And as you know, the doors to the school are warded. You are perfectly safe and we will continue to keep you as safe as possible, Bethany."

"Thank you, Professor." I stood up, still feeling scared, but I didn't want the Professor to know that. "I should go. I have... homework."

"Of course." Professor Singh stood then and walked to her office door, which she opened. "Thank you for telling me what occurred, Bethany. Do not think that we won't continue to research more and try to find who is behind this. You have nothing to worry about."

I gave her a half smile, but it didn't reach my eyes. "Thank you, Professor," I murmured as I hurried past her.

Once her door was shut, I ran down the hallway, not caring about the rules. I just wanted to get back to my room where I could break down behind my own dorm door.

CHAPTER 9
JAMES

I was still fuming over Professor Chalcedony's behavior when I reached my dorm room. I wondered how in the heck he'd managed to get hired with the attitude he held toward vampires. The man was clearly against us and would do everything in his power to destroy the newly built trust between the witches and us.

I dropped my books on my desk with a loud thunk. I wanted to break something or crush something, but I knew that would solve nothing. With a sigh, I pulled out my desk chair and sank into it.

"Bad day already, man?" Cory asked.

I rolled my eyes at him. "Be thankful you aren't Strigoi," I snarled.

"Whoa, what happened?" Cory asked, dropping his Manga comic to the bed and sitting up.

"History of the Magical World."

"O... kay. What about it?" Cory arched a brow in inquiry.

"The new prof. Professor Chalcedony," I snarled his name. "He hates vampires. He's making crap up about how vampires were the ones who began the witch trials in Salem."

"Huh?" Cory gave me a confused look.

"I know, right?" I rolled my eyes.

"Wasn't it the Puritans who started the witch trials?"

"Yes, sort of. It was two young girls who were from Puritan families, it spread from there." I sighed. "How am I supposed to connect vampires to them?" I asked incredulous, not expecting an answer.

"Hmmm, I don't know, man, lie?" Cory suggested.

"Whatever—" I started when my phone beeped. "Just a sec," I said, pulling out my phone and opening it. We didn't use them often here at the academy, but occasionally Bethany would send me something. Usually it was just funny things, memes and videos that made her laugh. I glanced down at the text.

Call me now! Bethany had sent.

I frowned. "Uh, I gotta call Bethany, something must have happened in her meeting with Professor Singh. Talk later?" I said looking up at Cory.

"Yeah, man. I'll head out to the commons, give you some privacy."

I nodded and hit the speed dial to call Bethany. A minute later, she answered.

"James?"

"What's wrong?" I asked, worried about the break in her voice.

"I... Professor Singh... Professor Singh... said..." she repeated, stuttering and sounding like she was on the edge of hysteria.

"Where are you?" I interrupted.

"My... my... room."

"I'll be there in a minute, open the window."

"Kay."

I shut my phone, flung open our dorm door and raced down the hall toward the doors that would lead to the courtyard. As soon as I got through the doors, I shifted and flew across the courtyard straight into Bethany's room. I shifted and pulled her into my arms as she began to sob.

I held her for several minutes before her wracking sobs quieted and she calmed down. "Bethany?" I said calmly, keeping my tone soft.

She sniffled, rubbing her face on my shirt, but I didn't care.

"Bethany, sweetheart, what happened?" I asked softly.

"I'm sorry." She swallowed and shook her head. "Professor Singh wanted to know about the Jiangshi. She... she said she, well they, her and the Dusk Knights, believe that it was brought here on purpose."

"What?" I asked in confusion. "Why would anyone do such a thing?"

"The Jiangshi was poisoned and she believes herded toward the bistro to get to *me*."

I felt as though my heart had exploded and shattered into a zillion pieces at her words. Someone had sent a vampire after the girl I loved! My body shook with rage at the thoughts playing through my mind. *How dare someone go after her and use a Jiangshi to do it!* I was breathing harshly and squeezing Bethany to the point that she yelped. I let go immediately, and tried to reel in my temper.

"James?" she said softly, her hand hesitantly reaching out to me. "James, are you okay?"

I took a few deep breaths, feeling more in control and nodded. Letting out a calming breath, I pulled her back into my arms and settled her under my chin. "Sorry, I'm okay. What else did the Professor say?"

"She says I'm safe here."

"You are," I acknowledged. "I will make sure you are."

"She's still investigating, trying to find out who is behind it."

"Good, good." I took another calming breath. "Let's go for a walk."

Bethany stepped away from me and wiped her eyes. "Do I look okay?"

I smiled. "You look beautiful."

Taking her hand, I pulled her out of her dorm room and together we went out to the courtyard and headed toward the clock tower. It was one of my favorite spots on campus and I wanted to be up high where I could see any threat coming toward us. We were more than half way there when I heard the ticking sound again that I'd heard on that first day back and I stopped walking.

"James?" Bethany questioned.

"Do you hear that?"

Bethany tilted her head and concentrated, picking up the sound. "Yeah, what is it? Is that the same sound from before? It sounds closer to us this time."

"Yeah, it does." I looked around curiously, it was getting dark, and the shadows around the buildings were even darker. Letting go of her hand, I moved forward a step or two toward where I thought the sounds were coming from and they got louder.

"James?" Bethany said softly, her voice sounding hesitant.

I took another step toward the clock tower. The sound was getting louder as I moved forward. Tick... tick... tick... tick... tick. It wasn't just getting louder. It was getting faster. Tick- tick- tick- tick.

Bethany hurried along behind me, pressing herself to my side, her fingers digging into my shirt, gripping it tightly. "Be careful..."

As we moved silently around the side of the clock tower toward the entrance, the shadows began to move, creeping closer toward us and began to loom several feet above our heads as it moved to greet us.

"Aaaaaaaaaaahhhh!" Bethany screamed as her eyes locked on the four creatures that separated from the shadows.

"Shadow Spiders!" I exclaimed as they clicked their pinchers and jumped at us.

CHAPTER 10

BETHANY

"Oh my god!" I screamed as one of the spiders moved forward on stilt like legs. There were four all together, three smaller ones and one large one. "James! What do we do?"

"I'll go for the big guy, can you hold off the other three with counter magic until I can get to them?" he asked quietly.

"I think so," I murmured as the ticking sound grew to a deafening pitch.

I began pulling energy from the shadows, allowing it to build inside me and then I forced it out in the direction of the smaller spiders. Two of the spiders flew back, their legs bent in awkward angles and didn't move, the third had jumped out of the way, so I repeated my actions, sucking in as much energy as I could and then releasing it directly at the spider. As it flew backwards, I saw James' body fly against the clock tower wall and drop to the ground.

"James!" I screamed, running toward him in a panic. "James!"

James lay on the ground, completely still. I knelt down next to him, aware the large spider was coming toward me. I felt his neck, looking for a pulse and soon found it. He was okay, just unconscious. I turned blocking him from the spider's ugly gaze. I stared at it defiantly, and put up a protective shield around us.

The black furry spider which stood about seven feet tall and about four feet wide clicked it's pinchers at me. It seemed to be watching me, waiting for me to do something or to move, but I stood my ground. After a few moments, the spider leapt in the air and came down directly on my shield, which zapped it and it flew through the air backwards, tumbling head over tail, but it tucked its legs in and rolled like a ball. It must have learned from the other spiders, because once it stopped it was back on its spindly legs creeping forward again.

I knelt down by James again, worried that if I dropped the shield the spider would attack him again. Shaking his arm, I said, "James, please wake up, please..." I quietly urged, my voice laced with my panic. "James, I don't know what to do, tell me what I need to do..." I fretted as I noticed the spider moving ever closer, but a bit more cautiously this time.

Biting my lip, I stood again, facing the spider. I silently began moving to my right, inching away from James, hoping the spider would follow me. The spider stopped for a moment, its buggy gaze on me, tracking my movements. It turned its body, slightly, as I moved and I knew I had its full attention. Slowly I made my way down the wall of the clock tower until I was at least five feet from James and the spider's attention was centered on me.

My heart was racing fiercely in my chest and I tried to calm it by drawing in some settling breaths. There was something familiar about this spider. It was smarter, behaved differently than the other three, almost as if it was smart. Or controlled. At that thought, I suddenly knew what was going on. The spider was a vessel for one of the Formless Ones! I'd fought one a couple of times the previous year, which was why this thing felt familiar.

I hadn't practiced any of my more powerful magic in months, thanks to being away all summer. Biting my lip again, I concentrated on bringing forth every ounce of magic within my being as the spider lunged toward my face. Then with a silent prayer to whoever might be listening, I blasted the spider and at the same time I opened a channel into the shadow energy and pulled it toward myself, drawing it in and cycling through my body and back at it. Thunder clashed and the whole sky lit up in a sheet of purple lightning that lasted several seconds.

As the counter magic hit the spider, it shook, vibrating with the amount of energy charging through it and then with a giant shudder it collapsed and a black misty fog lifted out of its eyes and rose up as the lightning flashed. It seemed to form a body for a fraction of a second and then, as the spider thudded to the ground, the Formless One zipped up into the dark sky and was gone.

With a sigh, I dropped to the ground on my knees in front of the spider. I panted, trying to catch my breath as I shook in relief that the battle was over. At least for now. I looked over my shoulder at James, and quickly crawled over to him, not sure my legs would lift me up enough for me to walk.

"James." I patted his cheek, softly at first, trying to wake him. "James!" I said forcefully, and patted a little harder.

James sat up, a hiss on his lips and his fangs out as he gripped my hand.

"James!" I called his attention to me and I saw him come back into himself.

"Bethany, what? What happened?" James let go of my hand as if it were a hot potato. "Are you okay? Where are the—" his head turned and he caught sight of the larger beast that had attacked us, "spiders. Did I?"

I shook my head.

"Did you?"

I nodded.

James pulled me into his arms and hugged me close. "Are you okay?" He pulled back and looked me over from head to toe.

"I'm alright. It didn't touch me. Are *you* okay?" I reached up and brushed hair off his forehead looking for any possible injuries.

He grasped my hand and smiled. "I'm fine now. Just got knocked out for a minute." He pulled me back into his arms again, holding me. "I'm so glad you are okay."

"Me too," I murmured. "James."

"Hmmm?"

"It was a Formless One."

I felt James go still, more still than anything should possibly be able to go. "Where is it now?"

"Gone. When I blasted the spider with every ounce of counter magic I could muster, I think it damaged the spider and it could no longer use it. It seeped from the creature and I tracked it for a second as the lightning flashed, but when the sky went dark again, I lost it as it zoomed away."

James nodded. "Could have been worse. I'm just glad you are alright."

I turned in his arms looking at the mess of spider bodies and wondered, "So what do we do about them?"

"Good question. We should probably take the large one to Professor Singh. Maybe she'll know what to do."

"You mean I'm gonna have to touch it?" I squirmed. "Bleck."

James chuckled. "It's an automaton, not a real spider. Real spiders don't grow this big. Come on." He moved forward, toward the creature and began folding all but two of the legs in toward its body. "Grab a leg and we'll pull it along behind us."

I reached out a hand, gripped one of the black fur covered legs, and shuddered. "This is not how I planned to spend my evening, just so you know."

James grinned at me. "Me either, sweetheart. Perhaps if we hurry this up, you can go with me to the nurse for a bite. After healing myself, I'm a bit drained."

I paused in pulling and made him stop too. "Maybe we should go there first, you need to eat, James—"

"I'm fine, Bethany, I promise. I just need a little bit," he interrupted me. "Besides, I wouldn't want anyone coming across this thing and getting frightened."

I snorted. "Yeah we were frightened enough for the entire student body." I grinned at him as we laboriously pulled the creature up the steps. "How are we getting this through the doors?"

"Sideways?" James suggested.

When we reached the doors, we both got on the same side and pushed so that it was up on its side instead of flat on its back. Then we rolled the spider through the doors and into the main hallway.

"Miss Welch, Mr. Barret! What exactly do you think you are doing with that?" Professor Zin asked marching toward us.

Curious students watched the scene we were unfolding. Silently I thanked whoever was watching over us that the halls weren't as crowded as usual. Still, within the next five minutes it would be all over school what had transpired or some version of it anyway.

With a sigh, I said, "We are taking it to Professor Singh. It attacked us near the clock tower, Professor. Actually there are four of them, but this is the largest one, and it was a vessel for—" I dropped my voice to barely a whisper, "a *Formless One*."

SOPHIE CASTLE

Professor Zin's eyebrows rose and then she pursed her lips, her hands on her tiny hips as she gazed up at us. "I see. Well then, carry on. Professor Singh will know what to do with it."

"Thank you, Professor." I smiled.

James, who had been leaning against the creature, resumed pulling the leg forward, and I returned to my leg and pulled as well. It took another ten minutes for us to reach Professor Singh's lab. We shoved it through the door and then went to her office and knocked.

"Miss Welch. Mr. Barret. To what do I owe the pleasure? I would have thought the two of you would be at your studies, as I am sure you both have reports to write?"

"We do, Professor. However we ran into a problem as we were out for a walk to clear our minds before we began work on our homework," I said with a hopeful smile.

"I'm sure that was what you were doing, Miss Welch." Professor Singh's lips quirked up a bit. "Now what sort of problem did you encounter?"

"We were outside the clock tower when we were attacked by four automatons," James said softly.

"Are you both alright?" she asked.

I nodded. "Yes, we're fine, well James was hurt, but he healed, he'll need blood, but we're mostly fine.

94

Professor, the large one, it was possessed by a Formless One. I was able to kill the automaton and the Formless One released it and got away, but we brought the automaton to your lab."

"How big is it?" she asked.

"Umm," I looked at James, "it's about what? Seven feet tall, when it's standing, right?"

"Yeah, about that." James nodded. "And about four feet wide."

"And you got it into the building?" Professor Singh arched her brows in surprise.

"Should we have left it?"

"No, no, you did the right thing. Though I don't imagine it went unnoticed."

"Errr, well..." I crinkled up my nose and shrugged. "No, it didn't. I think everyone knows about it by now."

"Wonderful." Professor Singh shook her head. "Well, let's go have a look, shall we?" She gestured toward the door.

We stepped back out to the hall and then followed her over to her lab.

"Ah, yes, definitely an automaton. I'll have to call in my knights." She looked over her shoulder at us. "You said there are four?"

I nodded. "Yes, the other three are smaller and

they were just automatons I guess. One blast and they were broken."

"Yes, I imagine they were just a distraction. This is the one we'll want to study closely." She walked around the beast and then returned to us. "Well, I will have my knights take care of the other three, and the two of you had best scurry. Reports won't write themselves. Mr. Barret, nurse first, please. Miss Welch, I think it's best you return to your dorm room now. After we spoke earlier, I think perhaps it would be wise to take precautions, so I will be adding additional wards to your window and door, so anyone wishing you harm will be unpleasantly surprised."

"Thank you, Professor," I murmured and looked over at James feeling pouty.

"In addition to that, I think perhaps it would also be a good idea to have you keep to the building, safe behind the school wards. At least until I have a chance to autopsy this creature and figure out what is going on."

I sighed. "Alright, Professor."

James smiled and kissed my temple. "I'll walk you to your dorm room." He wrapped his arm around my shoulders and guided me to the door. "Thank you, Professor Singh."

She nodded and waved her hand at us, dismissing us even with her attention already on the creature.

CHAPTER 11

JAMES

I couldn't believe the automaton had knocked me out. Of course, it had been possessed by a Formless One at the time, but still. I should have been able to at least stay on my feet. I worried a bit about how I'd woken and gripped Bethany, hissing at her. It was clearly not my finest moment.

"Hey," Bethany bumped her body into mine, "You okay?"

I chuckled. "I should be asking you that." I smirked at her. "I'm fine. I'm sorry for hissing at you."

Bethany grinned. "I didn't think you did it on purpose."

I grinned back. "Well, it was on purpose, just not directed at you." I laughed.

"I know." She laid her head on my shoulder. "I

wish we'd actually gotten to go sit at the clock tower. Now I have to do that stupid report for Chalcedony."

"Ugh. Don't remind me." I shook my head.

"How are we supposed to incorporate his bias into our text?" She frowned.

"Cory suggested we lie," I commented as we strolled down the hall toward her dorm room.

"What? Like we say that the girls were pawns of some vampire coven?"

I shrugged. "I guess."

"This is gonna be a really hard class if he keeps this stuff up." She frowned.

"We'll figure it out," I murmured. We'd reached her door and I dropped my arm from her shoulders, running my hand down her arm and taking her hand. I tugged her into me and held her, just breathing in her fresh sweet scent. She calmed me just by being there with me. I kissed her temple and leaned back a bit. "See you tomorrow morning for breakfast?"

She smiled and nodded. "Tomorrow, for breakfast." She opened her door and then turned and frowned. "And I forgot, Professor Singh said I have to stay in the building."

"I know. Maybe it won't be for long. We'll go see Professor Singh after classes and see what she's discovered. And I want to make sure she gets those wards up on your room as soon as possible. She is right, it would be safer to keep you in the building behind the wards. I can't imagine what I would do if I lost you to one of those attacks."

She sighed. "Me too, I mean I feel the same about you, too."

I grinned. "I knew what you meant." I kissed her nose and smiled at her.

She leaned forward and kissed me gently on my lips, a too brief brush of her lips before she said, "Good night."

With a sigh, I meandered down the hall and headed toward the nurse's station for my ration of blood. I hated that I had to rely on such things, but without it, I'd get sick. And I needed to be strong for her. To help keep her safe. I entered the nurse's station, which was set up with a small waiting room and desk. Deeper into the office were little cubicles with cloth curtains to hide us from any witches who might be there for other reasons. I signed into the book and took a seat in the waiting area.

"Mr. Barret?" the nurse, a pretty woman with blonde hair and bright blue eyes, asked. She wore a white dress that came down to her knees and a little white hat on her blonde hair. More like one of those nurses from the past. Probably because that was the era she was turned in and what was comfortable for her, I imagined.

"That's me." I stood.

"Did you not get enough earlier?" She frowned at me.

"It would have been, but I was out on the grounds and hit my head. I had to heal, so I need more."

"I see." The nurse nodded. "Follow me."

I followed her to the third cubicle and sat down in the cushioned seat. I watched as she unlocked a cabinet and wrote on a chart on the wall. "Do you have any AB positive?" I asked, it was my favorite and I hoped for a moment that I would be lucky enough to get a taste.

"I will check if we have any in the smaller bags after I check your vitals." She took my temperature and then my pulse. "Seventy-eight degrees and your pulse is a bit sluggish. I think maybe a medium bag. I'll be back." She returned her equipment to the cabinet, relocked it, and then left my cubicle, pulling the curtain closed.

I sighed and leaned back in my chair. I was almost asleep by the time she returned fifteen minutes later. I yawned and sat up.

"I'm sorry, I looked, but all I have is B positive. No AB positive."

"That's fine." I sighed, giving her a shrug.

She nodded and prepared the bag for me, pulling out a sterile scalpel, slitting the bag and inserting a straw. She handed it to me. "There you go. I'll return in ten minutes. Now, you drink all of that up."

"Yes, ma'am." I rolled my eyes as she turned her back to leave the cubicle.

I waited till the curtain closed before I leaned back and began drinking down the medium bag of B positive. It had a tang to it and a hint of power, which led me to believe that it was the blood of someone descended from a witch. Perhaps someone who didn't know they had power. The image of a red-headed girl, in her twenties floated through my mind. Occasionally when we ate, we got a read of whose blood we drank. The blood was always tested to make sure it was safe for us to consume. This girl's blood had no hints of drugs or alcohol, but it did have a sweetness to it that led me to believe she liked the occasional soda or cookie. The image hadn't been of someone who overindulged in anything, but someone who took care of her body. I appreciated that.

Once I'd finished, I licked my lips and ran my tongue over my teeth. I pressed a button on the side of the cabinet that lit up a little light outside to call the nurse discreetly. She arrived a moment later.

"Finished already?" she asked.

"Mmm, yes, thank you."

She pulled on latex gloves, and then took the emptied bag, removing the straw and deposited it in

SOPHIE CASTLE

a special receptacle for it. The straw she tossed in the trashcan along with her gloves. She handed me a small mirror. "Here you go."

I used the mirror to be sure I had gotten all signs of the blood off my teeth. "Thank you." I handed it back to her.

She opened the curtain and smiled. "You are free to go."

With a nod, I ducked out of the nursing station and headed back toward my dorm. The fresh blood had added a pep to my step and I was suddenly feeling wide awake. Probably a good thing, because as I rounded the corner the ethereal Librarian appeared in front of me, causing me to stop.

"Oh, hello."

The Librarian smiled and held a large tome out to me.

"What's this?" I questioned taking the book.

Pointing to the title, *Magical Uses of Automata,* the Librarian smiled again.

"Oh," I blinked, "I can take this with me?"

Again, the Librarian smiled, blue green eyes brightening in humor at me as they nodded. The Librarian was neither female nor male, and rarely spoke with words. They were always very mysterious.

"Will I need to return it in a certain time?" I asked.

The Librarian began to fade as they shook their head, and then they were gone.

I hefted the book up and sighed before continuing on to my room. As I pushed open the door, I noticed Cory once again stretched out on his bed. "Do you ever move?" I arched a brow.

"No." He laughed. "Seriously though, whats with the story of you and Bethany hauling a giant ugly spider into the school?"

Shaking my head, I dropped on my bed.

"What?" Cory looked at me. "Did something happen?"

"You could say that." I sighed and proceeded to tell him all about our battle and the aftermath of the event.

"Wow. Busy night." Cory grinned. "Better you than me, man."

I shook my head at him. "Did you already finish your homework?"

Cory nodded. "Still have that report, man?"

"Yeah." I frowned. "I'd better get started." I pushed off the bed and moved to the desk where I spent the next three hours b.s.-ing my way through the report.

Once I'd returned to my room, I'd worked on the report for Chalcedony, making up a tale about a non-existent vampire coven that had bespelled the Parris family's slave, Tituba into introducing the young girls into practicing 'magic'. They hadn't been real witches, though a few they accused had been. The tack I took was that the vampires wanted the Puritans to destroy all of the real witches in Salem, leaving them to rule the super-natural community. It was all a bunch of bologna, but it was what Professor Chalcedony wanted.

Helen came in as I was finishing it, around eleven. I tucked the report in my folder and closed my book. "Where have you been?" I asked with a smile.

"Oh, I met up with Finch and Quinn, we went to the diner for dinner instead of the cafeteria. Did you know there are giant spiders out in the courtyard?" She walked over to the window and peered out. "I hate spiders." She shivered. "They were dead, but still."

"Yeah, I killed them."

Helen blinked at me. "You?"

I nodded. "Yeah, they attacked James and me while we were on our way to the clock tower."

"And you just left them?" She put her hands on her hips and frowned at me.

I sighed. "Well, we took one to Professor Singh to study. She said she was going to send the Dusk Knights to take care of the rest."

"Hmmm. I suppose she did. They were out there too, walking all around them as well as the courtyard. It was kind of hard to figure out what they were doing exactly. Mostly it looked like they were standing there staring at the disgusting things."

"Well, I'm sure they will figure out what to do and get it all taken care of so no one else has to deal with them." I stood up and gathered my pjs and tooth-brush. "I'm heading to the bathroom. Are you coming?"

"I'll be there in a minute," Helen said over her shoulder as she stood at the window, still watching the Knights.

I nodded and trudged down the hall to the joint

bathroom shared by all the girls on our hall. I stepped into a stall and quickly changed, and then used the facilities, before going to the sink to wash my hands and then my face. Once that was done, I brushed my teeth. Helen still hadn't shown up by the time I was heading out. When I got to our room, she was nowhere to be seen. I shrugged.

"Maybe I missed her coming in," I murmured as I tossed my dirty clothes in the hamper and then climbed into bed.

A few minutes later, I fell into a deep slumberous sleep and began to dream.

❦

I WALKED THROUGH THE HALLWAYS OF THE SCHOOL, but no one else was around. I looked in every classroom door, and wondered where the students and professors were. I continued down the hallway toward the cafeteria, but there was no one there, no food was available in the kitchen. It was all deserted. Frowning I made my way down toward the vampire dorms to look for James.

Everything was eerily quiet. I couldn't hear anything that would lead me to believe there were any people around at all. I moved toward James' room and opened the door. Looking around, I could tell they weren't there, but comic books were strewn across Cory's bed and a book was open on James' desk.

I moved toward it and holding it at the page he had it opened to, I flipped the book to see the cover. Magical Uses of Automata.

"Huh, okay?" I said out loud just to see if I could. I sounded normal, but no one reacted to my comment. I turned back to the page to see what he'd been reading about.

Automata are self-operating machines. They are normally designed to automatically follow a predetermined arrangement of processes, or respond to predetermined commands. However with the inclusion of magic, generally dark magic, though, not always, an automaton can be given more power to think and act on the thoughts of their creators. Unlike human versions, these automata can actually be lethal and become vessels for Formless Ones to move about without detection.

"So the spiders are being controlled by a dark witch?" I murmured.

I stood up and looked around the room again. Not seeing anything else pulling at me, I left the room and returned to the cafeteria. While I stood there, my phone began to buzz. I picked it up and looked at the screen. It looked very odd, glowing a green and white with the words 'Mom's Calling' jarring across the screen.

The phone started beeping...

I AWOKE TO MY ALARM BEEPING FURIOUSLY AT ME. A pillow hit my face and I sat up and looked at Helen. "Sorry, I'll turn it off." I yawned and tossed her pillow back at her. I hit the button on the top of the clock and looked at it as I attempted to recall what I'd been dreaming about. Whatever it was, it hadn't been all that pleasant.

"Seriously? Six A.M.?" Helen groaned. "Why?"

"I'm meeting James for breakfast before class."

"Ugh." Helen gripped her pillow over her head and rolled on her side, burying herself deeper in her blankets. "Wake me when you get back."

"You're skipping breakfast?"

"Not hungry," Helen muttered. "Go away."

I shrugged, grabbed a fresh pair of jeans, a light blue top and undergarments before leaving the room. I returned fully dressed ten minutes later to hear her snoring loudly and I smiled. I ran a brush through my hair, pulling it back in a low ponytail, put on some cherry lip gloss, put on my socks and shoes and then picked up my books and left again.

I found a table on the outskirts of the room and set my books down then went to get my food. I thought it was sad that James didn't get to eat all the good food we did, and ended up grabbing far more than I intended. My plate was filled with extra helpings of scrambled eggs and fried potatoes as well as four slices of bacon. By the time I arrived back at my table, James was already there.

"Good morning, beautiful." He smiled at me as he pulled my chair out for me.

"Good morning," I commented, sitting. I took a bite of bacon, and chewed slowly. "Did you get your report done?"

James nodded. "Took me three hours, but yeah. Did you?"

"Mmmmhmmm," I murmured through my mouthful of eggs. After swallowing, I said, "Yeah, made up a non-existent vampire coven and said they bespelled Tituba into teaching the girls *magic*."

James nodded. "Great minds think alike," he smirked, "I did the same."

"Whoa, Bethany, hungry?" Terrance asked, dropping his tray on the table next to mine.

I rolled my eyes. "Good morning to you too, Terr." I shook my head at him. "You want some of this?" I gestured at my overflowing plate.

Terrance laughed. "Why'd you take it if you weren't gonna eat it?" he asked, snagging a slice of bacon off my plate.

"I was preoccupied as I was filling my plate, sue

me." I ate a few bites more of my eggs and potatoes and then shoved the tray forward.

"Did you guys hear about the spider infestation?" he asked as he moved his tray and grabbed mine.

"Infestation?" James asked.

"Yeah, I was out with Jodie last night and the Dusk Knights were all over the place rounding up bodies of giant spiders. Somebody brought a really big one in to Professor Singh too."

I swallowed my smile and looked at James.

"That was us."

Terrance's jaw dropped, bacon falling out.

"Ewww, close your mouth, Terr." I laughed.

Terrance picked up the bacon and finished eating it. "So what happened?"

"We were just walking and the spiders came out of nowhere. Bethany hit them with her magic and killed them," James summarized our adventure from the night before, making it sound less dangerous than it was.

I arched a brow at him, wondering if he was purposely not telling the whole of it.

"Wow, cool. I'm sorry we missed out on the fun," he commented as he began to shovel the rest of the food into his mouth.

"You finished?" James asked me with a smile.

"Yeah. Terrance, I'll see you later. Oh, I'll take your tray since you've got mine."

Terrance nodded and continued to eat.

"See ya later." I picked up the tray with the bowl of cereal and emptied it in the trash, setting the tray on top. I turned back to grab my books, but James already had them and handed them to me. "Thanks."

He leaned in and kissed my cheek. "You seem a little distracted. You okay?" he asked, studying me.

"Yeah. Just had this weird dream that I can't quite remember. It's all fuzzy, but I feel like I am supposed to remember it."

"That is strange." He smiled at me. "I bet if you stop trying to think about, it will return to you when you need it."

"Okay, you're probably right."

He leaned in and kissed me again. "I'll see you in Chalcedony's class, okay?"

I nodded and then we both went in opposite directions. I ran down the corridor to my dorm, realizing I'd forgotten that Helen had said to wake her and I hoped she was already awake. I opened the door to find her still in bed.

Crap.

I shook her shoulder. "Helen!"

Helen snorted into her pillow and flapped a hand at me.

"Helen, we have twenty minutes to get to class! Wake up!"

Helen rolled over and blinked. She looked at me blankly and then turned to the clock on the night table. "Oh my god! Why did you let me sleep so late!" She sprang from the bed and began pulling clothes from her dresser. "Now I don't have time to shower! And look at my hair!" she squealed. "What am I going to do?"

"Take a breath, Helen, get dressed, brush your hair and let's go!"

"This is your fault, you know," she mumbled through her top. "I had nightmares all night about those spiders!"

"How is that my fault?" I frowned at her as she tugged on a pair of jeans.

"I don't know. It just is. Weird stuff always happens around you. First that Jiangshi and now spiders. What's going to be next?" She stared at me a moment before pulling the brush through her hair. She sighed. "I'm sorry. I shouldn't blame you. I'm just mad I overslept." She turned to me frowning. "Forgive me?"

I gave her a half smile. "Sure. We better go now, Professor Singh won't like it if we're late."

"Right!" She picked up her books and practically ran to our class.

৩⁂৩

THE DAY SEEMED TO BE SPEEDING BY. Chalcedony's class was going by without any incidents, but then, he'd just lectured for the last hour and a half about the perceived slights the vampires perpetrated against the witches of the past. I was finding it all rather boring. Glancing around the room, I knew the Strigoi in the class were probably pissed off at him, judging by the hateful looks that they were giving him.

I turned my gaze on James. I wanted to reach over and calm him, but I knew I'd get into trouble with Chalcedony. James looked to be very on edge, his jaw tight and the muscle jumping in his cheek with each derogatory word Chalcedony spat. I willed him to take some deep calming breaths and remember that Chalcedony was a professor and he couldn't attack him.

As soon as the bell rang, James sprang from his seat as if his pants were on fire. I gathered up my books, determined to follow him and meet him in the hall, but by the time I got there, he was nowhere to be seen. He hadn't even waited for me.

I fumed as I trudged to my next class. "Stupid bigoted professor," I muttered.

I wasn't mad at James for leaving me behind. I

knew he'd had to get out of there before he did something he'd regret. I feared there would be an altercation before the semester was over. Shaking my head I entered my next class. Math. The boring normal high school kind of class, nothing fun or interesting about it, just numbers. Well, okay it wasn't totally uninteresting. I had always enjoyed math, I was just not particularly interested in it right then. I really wanted to go find James and make sure he was all right.

As I was pulling out my books, I felt my phone buzz in my pocket. I peeked up at the Professor at the front of the room, and noticing his back was turned, writing on the board, I slipped the phone out of my pocket and looked at it.

Sorry for leaving you in the dust, I had to get out of there. <3 James

Peeking up at the professor, I took the moment to text, *I understand. <3*

My phone buzzed again silently.

Meet me by Professor Singh's lab after class?

I wondered if he wanted to see what Professor Singh had found out about the spider. I wanted to know too. Especially how a Formless One had been able to possess it. Something about that seemed familiar, but I didn't know why.

Be there after class. Xoxo, I sent back.

"Miss Welch? Do I need to confiscate your phone?"

I glanced up at Professor Marks and felt my cheeks heat. "No, sir. Sorry, sir." I turned the phone off and put it back in my pocket.

I managed to sit through the rest of class and take notes over the next algebraic formula without drawing any more attention to myself. When the bell rang, I gathered up my books and headed out of the door.

I rounded a corner and headed down the hallway that held the classrooms of the rest of our regular classes, English classes, all the different math classes and sciences, and then took the next right toward Professor Singh's lab. The academy was a maze of hallways that had taken me weeks to figure out last year, and as big as the fictional *Hogwarts* of the *Harry Potter* world.

James was waiting for me next to the door. He was leaned back against the wall, looking down at his phone. As I approached, he looked up and smiled. Shoving his phone in his back pocket, he moved toward me.

"Hi," he said softly as he brushed a lock of my hair off my cheek and tucked it behind my ear.

"Hi, yourself." I grinned. "Feeling better?" I asked.

"Much, thank you. That professor is going to drive me to do something I shouldn't."

I glanced up at his face. A look of irritation flickered in his eyes and I was sure it wasn't aimed at me, but at Professor Chalcedony. I reached up and drew his eyes down to mine and then lifted up on my toes and brushed a kiss across his lips. "It's two hours of the day. He doesn't matter. Who cares if we pass that irritating class? We can take it again with a different professor next year if we have to. You just have to keep your cool for the rest of the semester and then we can go to Professor Zin and get out of the class."

James arched a brow. "You think she'll let us out of it?"

I shrugged. "Probably. Well maybe not me, but you have a good case for being let out of the class with Chalcedony's bigotry. If all of the Strigoi go in and complain and take proof, like that essay he assigned, I am sure she will see reason."

"I'll talk to the others. I'm sure they are as frustrated with him as I am." James pulled me to him and kissed me.

"No PDA in the hallway," Finch called from down the hall as he approached us.

I turned and grinned at him. "Hey Finch, what's up?"

"Nothing, I was just headed back to the witch commons for a little R and R. You coming?"

"No, thanks though, we've got an appointment with Professor Singh."

Finch put his feathered hands on his hips and got a serious expression on his face. "Anything I should know about?"

James chuckled. "I think we can handle it, but thanks though."

"Well, if you're sure. I kind of miss the practice we set up last year. I was hoping maybe you were going to start another club for this year."

"Bethany is basically under house arrest right now, so that's a no, for now anyway. Until we can figure out what's going on."

"Ah, yeah? House arrest? What did you do?" Finch frowned at me.

"I didn't do anything!" I huffed.

"She didn't, it's more that she's under attack. At least we think that might be what's going on."

"Those giant spiders?"

I nodded. "Yeah, and the Jiangshi before school started."

"Ah, yeah. That bites. Well, if you need backup, you know where to find me." Finch gave us a salute. "Catch you two later."

"Bye, Finch." I smiled after him as James pulled me back in his arms.

"I'm glad you've got friends like him," he commented.

I nodded. "Me too." I stepped back and adjusted my books.

"Ready to see what Professor Singh discovered?" James asked with a smile. He held out his hand for me.

I nodded and took his hand. Together we entered the lab.

"Oh, good. I was just going to send for you both," Professor Singh commented as we approached her.

She pulled off her glasses and walked with us over to the now dismembered and pried open carcass of the spider. Half of its insides were on the table next to it and covered in a sickly green liquid that had congealed.

"So it was a living creature?" I asked.

"In a way, Miss Welch." Professor Singh nodded at me.

"What do you mean?" I frowned at her and then turned back to look at the spider again.

"What I mean is that this creature is, as you suspected, Mr. Barret, indeed an automaton. The interesting thing is, if you look here—" She pointed at the mouth of the creature. Here, take a closer look.

When she said the word 'automaton' I recalled what I'd read in my dream. That the automata were creations that when imbued with magic, could think and act on their creator's thoughts. I shivered as I moved up to the table and took the offered lab glasses and without knowing why, exactly, I slid them on.

"Just in case, wouldn't want either of you to injure something as vital as your eyes."

I looked over at James as he too slid a pair of the clear thick glasses over his eyes. Both of us moved closer to the creature without touching it we peered into the face cavity and noticed what Professor Singh was talking about.

"Well that is rather terrifying. A vampire automaton spider?" James questioned.

"Oh! I didn't notice those teeth last night," I said a beat later, staring at a set of fangs.

"No, you wouldn't have until it was too late and they were buried in you. We had to cut away a bit of the mouth area right here, to get in there." She pointed to the section that would have covered the fangs. "After testing, we discovered they are venomous." She paused and stared directly at me as if waiting for my reaction.

It took a moment and then it dawned on me. "The Jiangshi."

"Indeed, Miss Welch. The Jiangshi's lower half was covered in bites from this particular creature. I think whoever was controlling it had it bite the Jiangshi. Once they knew when you entered the area, they sent the Jiangshi down the path to encounter you. This had to take quite a bit of planning and they must have had people watching out for you in order to time it correctly. So, I imagine, when the Jiangshi didn't kill you as they'd hoped it would, they sent the spider itself after you."

I swallowed hard and blinked at her. "Why?" I looked up at her and frowned. "I don't understand. I mean I haven't even learned how my magic really works, how can anybody want to kill me? Why are they doing this to me?"

Professor Singh sighed. "As I am sure you are aware, Miss Welch, you are more powerful than almost every witch around. Whoever this is, they are afraid that once you learn more, you'll take over the world, or some other such nonsense." She patted my shoulder. "In other words, they fear what will happen to themselves and plan to destroy it or in this case, you, before you can get to them."

"But I never asked for all of this power. And I

don't want to hurt anyone with it. Witch or vampire or even human." I frowned.

James hugged me to his side and kissed my temple. "I know," he said softly.

"I know. And I am sure all of us here will do our best to protect you." Professor Singh smiled, but it was more sad than happy.

"Professor, could this all be related to the Shadow Society?" I asked hesitantly.

Professor Singh tilted her head and then sighed. "I suppose it's possible, Bethany. But I don't see how they could get into the school. We're pretty protected here."

I nodded, but frowned.

"Come, let's go get those wards up on your room before someone decides to try something else."

I nodded again. "Thank you, Professor." I smiled at her. "Do you..." I stopped, considering my words. "I'm just wondering, do you think, whoever it is that is doing this, is here, in the school?"

Professor Singh gave me a considering look. "Is it possible? I suppose it *is*, possible. However all of us here are committed to making this alliance between witches and vampires work, so I cannot imagine someone here deliberately and intentionally going after you or exposing the humans to such danger as the Jiangshi." She frowned. "The problem is, I could be wrong, Miss Welch. Which is why I want to put up the wards on your room. I want you to have a specific safe place away from harm." She peered at me as if she was trying to assure me. "The school is warded, yes, but these wards will be more precise and keep anyone who intends to harm you out of your room."

"I understand, Professor, thank you for doing this." Sighing, I followed her down the hallway with James at my side.

CHAPTER 13

BETHANY

We made our way through the maze of hallways and up a flight of stairs to my dorm hallway. James held my hand the whole way and it comforted me greatly. When we reached my dorm room, I pushed open the door to a surprised Helen.

"Uh, what's going on?" she asked, seeing Professor Singh.

"Nothing to worry about, dear. I'm just going to add some additional wards to your room, to make sure no harm comes to either of you." She smiled and began to work some magic weaving it over the window and the sill.

"Professor, will the ward still hold if I open the window?" I asked curiously. I wanted to be sure that I could let James into the room in his owl form if I needed to without upsetting the wards.

"Yes, they will work fine. Nothing will able to pass the barrier of the ward if it intends harm to either of you."

I watched the magical ward snap into place as she turned toward the door and performed the same actions, weaving a strong magic upon it as well. Just before the spell snapped into place, I heard that tick, tick, tick sound again that told me spiders were close. "James!"

"I hear it," he acknowledged.

Then a screeching sound occurred from under my bed and two spiders about the size of small dogs scuttled out, spun around, hopped a time or two and then collapsed, shriveling into mere husks of their bodies.

Helen screamed at the sight and fainted, and if James hadn't been as fast as he was, she would have hit the floor. He picked her up and laid her on the bed.

"Ridiculous girl," Professor Singh said with a sigh. She turned her gaze back to the spiders. "Well, this does indeed prove that you are the one on the hot seat, my dear." She patted my arm. "No need to worry though. These wards will keep you safe. I think it would be best if neither of you mention the wards."

She looked back at Helen and then to us. "Will she gossip about it?"

I shook my head, but I wasn't really sure. "I don't think so."

"I could wipe her memory—"

"No, no, I'll talk to her," I cut in. I knew what it felt like to have your memory messed with and it wasn't a great feeling. "Thank you, Professor."

Professor Singh smiled. "Very well. I'll leave it to you. Might I again suggest that you try not to venture out of the building without someone to accompany you? I know being under house arrest isn't fun, but it really is for your safety, Miss Welch."

"Yeah, that won't be happening. I might just lock myself in here forever where it's safe." I crossed my arms over my chest and rubbed my hands up my arms, frowning.

"Oh, I don't think that will be necessary, my dear. Just take extra precautions and you should be fine."

"Thank you, Professor. I won't let her go out without me or someone else to protect her," James commented.

"I'll leave you to it then." She nodded, checked her wards once more and then turned toward the door.

Helen picked that moment to wake up and then looking around the room, she noticed the spider husks. "Oh my god!" She scooted back on her bed and pressed herself against the headboard in a ball.

"Helen, they're dead, they can't hurt you," James said quietly.

Her eyes flashed to him and then she moved forward slightly, peering over the edge of the bed. "Are there any more?"

"No, if there were, they would be just as shriveled up and dead as these two." Professor Singh pointed to the bodies.

"What are we going to do about them?" I asked.

"I'll take care of them."

"I'll help you, Mr. Barret. We can take them back to my lab."

James picked one up by its shriveled legs and Professor Singh did the same.

"Stay here, do not leave this room, either of you." James looked between us both.

"We won't leave," I replied, knowing it was only because he wanted to be sure that Helen kept her mouth shut about the wards.

"I'll be right back."

Helen nodded.

I sat down on my bed and sighed.

"Bethany?"

"Hmmm?" I looked over at her.

"I don't think... I don't think I can stay in here."

"But we're safe in here, and we told James we'd stay." I didn't understand her sudden panic after the threats had been removed.

"I-I know, but... I can't sleep in here. I won't get any sleep."

I frowned. "Where will you go?"

Helen shrugged. "Maybe in with Luci and Porta. They'll make room for me."

I sighed. "So you're gonna just leave me here?"

She shrugged again. "They're after you," she said softly, her eyes sad, and still panicked.

I felt my eyes begin to tear up. I swallowed hard and nodded. I couldn't blame her, not really. "While you were, indisposed, Professor Singh asked that we not tell anyone about the added wards. Can you... can you not tell anyone, please?"

Helen nodded as she skirted around her bed, avoiding the area where the spiders had died. She pulled a bag out of the closet and began filling it with clothes and toiletries. "If... if I need anything else, I'll knock, but I'm not coming in here again, not without others with me."

"I understand," I murmured as James returned.

Helen looked at both of us, picked up her bag and scurried out of the room.

"Where is she going?"

Tears spilled down my cheeks. "To Porta and

Luci's room. She won't stay here." My voice broke as I spoke.

James gathered me in his arms and held me as I sobbed. I felt like a blubbering mess. It seemed like all I had done since arriving back at school was cry, but I was frightened and alone except for James and he'd have to go back to his room soon.

"Do you want me to stay?" he murmured, picking up on my thoughts somehow.

I nodded. "Please?"

He smiled. "Of course. Let me text Cory. I won't tell him about the wards, but I will tell him about the spiders."

"Okay."

I waited as he texted Cory and then he shoved his phone in his pocket again.

"Are you hungry? We could go get some dinner and then come back here."

"Not really, but I guess I should." I wiped my face. "Maybe a stop at the bathroom first."

James smiled. "Come on, let's go get you cleaned up."

He took my hand and led me down the hall to the bathroom, waiting patiently outside while I ran in and washed my face. I took a moment to really look at myself. My eyes were still slightly puffy and my cheeks were a bit pink, but overall, I looked okay. I hoped no one else would be able to tell that I'd been crying my eyes out.

"Ready?" James asked as I came out.

He held his hand out to me and I took it like a life line. We made our way to the cafeteria and I picked a BLT sandwich and some chips up to eat. James didn't leave me alone for a second. Together we chose a table away from the windows and closer to the professor's hallway. I picked at the sandwich, pulling it apart and eating it in pieces between chips. When I finished, James threw the rest away and we quietly headed back to my room.

We settled on my bed, sitting against the headboard. James picked up my copy of *Harry Potter Chamber of Secrets* and began to read it to me as I snuggled into his chest. I fell asleep somewhere around the time Harry opened the chamber in the sinks of the girls' bathroom.

CHAPTER 14

JAMES

Aftter leaving Professor Singh's lab, we headed to Bethany's dorm. I knew Bethany was worried, and I'd seen her eyes light up in the lab when the professor had told her about the automaton. I had to wonder if she knew more about them than I'd thought.

Bethany opened her dorm door and as we moved into the room, Helen turned toward us, a concerned look on her face. "Uh, what's going on?" she asked.

"Nothing to worry about, dear. I'm just going to add some additional wards to your room, to make sure no harm comes to either of you." Professor Singh smiled at her and turned toward the window. I could see her hands fill with magic as she started weaving it over the window and its frame.

"Professor, will the ward still hold if I open the

window?" Bethany asked and I noticed the increase in her heart beat.

Looking at her and meeting her eyes, I could tell she wanted to know if I'd be able to come in that way. I smiled at her, knowing the answer before Professor Singh could reply.

"Yes, they will work fine. Nothing will able to pass the barrier of the ward if it intends harm to either of you."

As the wards began to snap into place I heard a distinct *tick- tick- tick.*

"James!"

"I hear it," I commented, pulling her against me to protect her.

Then a screeching sound occurred from under her bed and two spiders, not much bigger than Yorkshire Terriers scurried out and turned in circles as if confused. They managed to leap in the air, about knee high, and then buckled, withering away into spider husks.

Helen screamed at the sight and fainted, but I caught her before she fell to the floor and then laid her on the bed.

"Ridiculous girl," Professor Singh said with a sigh. She turned her gaze back to the spiders. "Well, this does indeed prove that you are the one on the hot seat, my dear." She patted Bethany's arm. "No need to worry though. These wards will keep you safe. I think it would be best if neither of you mention the wards." She looked back at Helen and then to us. "Will she gossip about it?"

"I don't think so." Bethany looked almost sure, but she shook her head in the negative.

"I could wipe her memory—"

"No, no, I'll talk to her," Bethany cut in. "Thank you, Professor."

Professor Singh smiled. "Very well. I'll leave it to you. Might I again suggest that you try not to venture out of the building without someone to accompany you? I know being under house arrest isn't fun, but it really is for your safety, Miss Welch."

"Yeah, that won't be happening. I might just lock myself in here forever where it's safe." Bethany crossed her arms over her chest and rubbed her hands up and down her arms, frowning.

"Oh, I don't think that will be necessary, my dear. Just take extra precautions and you should be fine."

"Thank you, Professor. I won't let her go out without me or someone else to protect her," I promised. I would stay by her side as much as I could, and if I couldn't be there, I would make sure she had somebody with her.

"I'll leave you to it then." Professor Singh nodded.

She looked over her wards once more and then turned toward the door.

"Oh my god!" Helen screamed and scooted back on her bed. She pressed herself against the headboard in a ball.

"Helen, they're dead, they can't hurt you." I said the words softly, but I really wanted to roll my eyes at her drama. They weren't going to harm her now, obviously.

Her eyes flashed to me and then she moved forward slightly, peering over the edge of the bed. "Are there any more?"

"No, if there were, they would be just as shriveled up and dead as these two." Professor Singh pointed to the bodies.

"What are we going to do about them?" Bethany asked.

"I'll take care of them." I sighed.

"I'll help you, Mr. Barret. We can take them back to my lab."

I picked one up by its shriveled legs and Professor Singh did the same.

"Stay here, do not leave this room, either of you." I looked between them both.

"We won't leave," Bethany replied.

"I'll be right back," I promised.

Professor Singh and I carried the creatures as

closely to us as we could, as we tried not to attract attention.

"I am anxious to see if these smaller ones have the same interior as the large one."

"Do you think they have fangs and venom like the large one?" I asked.

"I would imagine so. Otherwise what would be the point of stashing them in Miss Welch's room?" she replied.

That was what worried me. That someone was able to get into the building, into her room with those things unseen and plant them under her bed. "Professor, how were they able to get them in there like that?"

"That is a very good question, Mr. Barret. I have been wondering the same myself. They should not have been able to breach the wards on any of the building's doors if they had the intention of hurting Miss Welch. So it would seem that these particular automatons were created within the school."

My heart dropped to my stomach. "Then that means someone in the building *is* behind the attacks."

Professor Singh glanced at me and pursed her lips at the implication. "I am aware, Mr. Barret."

"Is it possible Bethany is right and that whoever it is behind all of this is a member of the Shadow Society?"

She glanced at me again and pressed her lips in a firm line. "Yes, that is a very real possibility but I don't want to pursue that line yet unless we have to. The Shadow Society is nothing to mess with Mr. Barret."

I nodded.

We pushed into the lab and she drew me toward the back where we placed the bodies.

"I think it might be best if we keep that part to ourselves for now. Miss Welch is a smart girl, I have a feeling she already knows, but it may be best not to bring it up. She's safer now. And I will re-ward the doors of the building with additional wards aimed at keeping her safe. For now, do you think you can keep an eye on her? I have a feeling that roommate of hers will leave her on her own and I fear she will flee back to the vampire dorms."

"Can she? We would be happy to have her, Professor."

Professor Singh smiled. "I know you would. However, where she is now really is the safest place for her right at the moment because we don't know where the threat is coming from. Perhaps you could stay with her through the holiday weekend and that will be enough to make her comfortable in her own room."

"If you think that is best, Professor," I agreed.

"And James," she said, stopping me as I headed toward the lab door.

"Yes, Professor?" I looked up at her curiously.

"Thank you both for not turning this into a witch or vampire hate crime. I really do think it has more to do with Bethany's power more than anything."

I nodded. "I agree, Professor."

Professor Singh nodded and gave me a grateful smile. "Keep her distracted this weekend. It's the best thing for her."

"I will." I headed out of the lab and back to Bethany's room.

When I opened the door and walked through the ward I could feel it, just a slight tingle of the magic.

"I understand," Bethany said to Helen, a sad look on her face.

I glanced between them and noticed Helen had been packing. I knew she wouldn't stick around. It appeared the professor and I were right.

Helen looked at both of us, picked up her bag and scurried out of the room.

"Where is she going?" I asked, just to be sure I wasn't misinterpreting things.

Tears pooled in Bethany's eyes and began to slip down her cheeks. "To Porta and Luci's room. She won't stay here."

I pulled her to me, cradling her against my chest

as she cried. I rubbed soothing circles on her back, attempting to calm her. I tried to come up with a plan in order to distract her, as Professor Singh had suggested. "Do you want me to stay?" I murmured, keeping my voice low and quiet. The last thing we needed was a passing student outside of the room to overhear our conversation.

"Please?" Bethany peered up at me, her lip trembling as she nodded.

I smiled. This girl had me wrapped around her little finger, she just didn't realize it fully how much I would give up for her. "Of course. Let me text Cory. I won't tell him about the wards, but I will tell him about the spiders."

"Okay."

Hey man, Bethany was nearly attacked again by some more of those spiders. I have permission to stay with her through the holiday weekend. Will you drop by her room with my pjs and a change of clothes for me? Thanks. - James

Waiting a moment, Cory sent a text back and I read it.

Sure man, that sucks. She okay? - Cory

Yeah, just shook up a bit. See ya after midnight, gonna try and get her to get some sleep. I think she needs it. - James

K, sounds good. - Cory

I shoved my phone in my pocket again and asked,

"Are you hungry? We could go get some dinner and then come back here."

"Not really, but I guess I should." She wiped her face and gave me a tremulous smile. "Maybe a stop at the bathroom first."

I smiled, glad to see her coming back to herself. "Come on, let's go get you cleaned up."

We walked down the hall to the bathroom, and I waited outside the doors for her. Leaning back against the wall, I pulled my phone back out. Thinking, I sent out another text.

Hey Jodie, Bethany had another run-in with some spiders and I want to make sure she's safe, you on board for a little distraction in the near future? - James

Sure, what do you have in mind? - Jodie

I've got the weekend covered, and most days after classes, but maybe next weekend or something? Think you can plan something? - James

Of course! I'm on it! - Jodie

Bethany came out of the bathroom looking better now that she'd washed her face. Her eyes weren't as puffy and she was smiling as she approached me.

"Ready?" I asked holding out my hand.

She took it and if I weren't a vampire, I think she might have fractured my fingers with her grip. We made our way to the cafeteria and she picked up some kind of sandwich and a bag of chips as I walked through the line with her. I gently led her to a table near the professor's hallway.

I stayed silent, just watching her as she took tiny bites of the sandwich and ate just a few of the chips. When she pushed the plate away, indicating she was finished, I picked up the plate and threw the rest away. Taking her hand, I quietly walked with her back to her room.

I wondered if she'd want to go change and get more comfortable, but she must have decided not to, because she pulled me down to her bed and laid her head on my chest. I picked up her copy of *Harry Potter Chamber of Secrets* and held it to see if she wanted me to read to her. She nodded against my chest, so I began to read. She fell asleep about a third of the way in and I smiled.

Glancing at the clock, I noticed it was nearing midnight. Cory would be here with my things any moment. I gently moved her from my chest to her pillow and then stood up and stretched. I heard the sound of footfalls coming down the hallway and moved to the door, opening it softly to see if it was Cory.

I stepped out and smiled, seeing it was him. "Hey Cors. Thanks for bringing these."

"No problem. Bethany okay?" he asked.

"Yeah, she's sleeping. Spent the last several hours

reading to her." I smiled thinking about the book. I'd read the series numerous times and every time I did, I discovered something new to love about them.

"That's good at least. What are you two doing tomorrow?" he asked as I took the clothes from him.

"Not sure yet. I think we'll play it by ear, see how she's feeling, you know?"

"Yeah man. I get it. She must have been pretty freaked."

"You could say that, but the girl's brave, she did her best not to show it. She's more broken up because her roommate ditched her."

"Well that sucks. I was wondering how you were getting away with staying in there." Cory chuckled.

"Singh gave me permission. Just for the weekend though."

"What's she gonna do during the week? She coming back over with us?"

I shook my head. "No, I don't think so. She had special circumstances last year, this year, well, it's just different. Professor Singh thinks she's safer here." I pointed my thumb over my shoulder at the door.

"Is that—" Cory's hand reached toward the door.

"Don't." I grabbed his hand. "It's exactly what you think, but we aren't letting anyone know." I glanced up and down the hallway to be sure we were alone.

Cory pulled his hand back and nodded. "The

encounter happened here?" he commented looking incredulous.

I nodded.

"You're right, she's brave. I don't think I'd be staying anywhere I encountered those things."

I smirked at him. "Okay, you better go, keep your mouth shut about this, okay?"

"Yeah, sure, man." Cory nodded again. "See you later, okay?"

"Yeah." I waited for him to move down the hall and then I re-entered the room.

Seeing Bethany was still asleep, I quickly changed into my sleep pants and a t-shirt. I pulled an extra blanket from her closet, sat down on the bed and then pulled the blanket over both of us. Closing my eyes, I laid back and enjoyed the feeling of her pressed to my side.

I WAS GLAD IT WAS SATURDAY AND WE DIDN'T have to get up early and rush off to classes. I'd spent most of the night holding Bethany as she slept and didn't really get much sleep myself, not that I needed a whole lot. At around nine A.M. I felt her wake, her face pressed to my chest, a smile on her lips.

"Good morning, beautiful." I kissed the top of her head.

"What time is it?" she murmured sleepily.

"Going on nine, are you hungry?"

She nodded against my chest.

"Then you'd best get up and showered before they shut down the kitchen to start prepping for lunch."

Bethany sighed. "Fine." Reluctantly she raised up and stretched her arms above her head as she arched her back. She slid her feet to the floor and stood up. Glancing at me she said, "When did you change into sleepwear?"

I smiled. "While you slept. Cory brought me some stuff. Figured I might as well be comfortable. You mind?"

She blushed and shook her head. "You aren't going to stay in those, are you?" she asked.

Grinning, I said, "Depends on what you want to do today."

"Breakfast, then beyond that? I haven't any idea."

"Then I might just stay in these." I grinned and pulled on my shoes.

She nodded and then stared hesitantly at the door as if she wasn't sure she wanted to leave the room.

"Want me to look first?" I asked, arching a brow.

She nodded and then went to gather her clothes as I moved to the door. I opened it and peeked my head out into the hallway. I didn't see anyone or anything around, so I gently closed the door and smiled at her.

"All clear."

She took a breath and smiled. "Good."

Taking her hand, I walked to the bathroom with her and again waited outside the room while she showered and changed.

Together we walked to the cafeteria. Once again I went through the line with her as she picked up a waffle, two hardboiled eggs, some sausage and the syrup as well as a glass of milk. Smiling, I carried the tray for her and we sat down at the same table we'd sat at the evening before.

"So, what are you thinking we should do today?" I asked as she ate.

She shrugged and looked down at her food. "I wish I could go outside."

"We could try..."

She shook her head. "No, I don't want to chance it."

"What if others are out there, I don't think anyone will attack if there is a large group of us. We could get a group together and maybe play some basketball, or maybe Frisbee?"

She giggled. "Frisbee?"

I laughed. "Yeah, well, trying to think of something we could do with a group."

Smiling she bit into her sausage. "How about we see who is available and then decide?"

"That sounds like a good plan. Though now I'll have to change." I chuckled.

Bethany blushed. "Okay. I bet everyone is in the commons, how about you walk with me there, then you can go back to my room and change and I'll see who might want to go out with us?"

"Sounds like a plan." I kissed her nose, picked up her tray and emptied it for her. I turned back and took her hand, pulling her up and we walked to the witch common room. "You'll be okay?"

"I think so." She nodded and squeezed my fingers. "Just don't be too long."

"I'll be just like *the Flash*, you won't even know I'm gone." I grinned.

CHAPTER 15

BETHANY

"**H**ey guys." I smiled as I approached my friends tentatively.

"Hi, Bethany," Finch looked up from his video game and smiled, "what's up?"

Porta, Luci and Helen glanced at me too and smiled.

You okay? Helen told us about the attacks. Luci looked at me curiously.

I'm fine, James has been with me, so I'm doing okay, I replied with a smile. I'm sorry it's driven Helen into your space though.

It's okay. It's a larger room, so there's room for her. I'm worried about you though, you gonna be okay on your own?

Yeah, thanks.

Okay. Luci smiled.

"So?" Finch asked, raising his eyebrows at me.

"Right, well, as you know I am sort of under house arrest?"

"Yep, we're aware." Finch nodded. "And?"

"Well, I have permission to go out of the building if there are others around..."

"And?" Quinn looked up at me and arched a brow.

"And James—"

"What Bethany is trying to ask is would you all want to come outside with us and maybe play a pickup game of basketball or something?" James finished for me and kissed my cheek. "Told you I'd be like *the Flash*." He grinned as he wrapped his arms around me.

Finch set his game controller down. "Yeah, okay, I'm in."

Quinn and Terrance put their controllers down too and nodded. "Sure, we're in."

"I think I'll pass," Helen said quietly.

Porta looked at Luci who nodded. "We'll go with you."

I smiled. "Thank you." I let out a relieved breath.

"I'll grab a ball and meet you guys all out on the court," Finch commented.

I nodded.

"You sure you don't want to come, Helen?" Porta encouraged her with a look.

Helen seemed to think about it, looking

between us all and then with a small sigh, she said, "Okay, I'll come." She stood and then walked close to Quinn as we all headed to the east side of the building and then out to the basketball courts. "You know, we could do this in the gym... behind the wards."

"Kind of defeats the purpose of getting Bethany out of the building though, don't you think?" Quinn argued.

"Yeah, I guess," she muttered.

Finch showed up minutes later and we all went out onto the court. We split up into teams, four on four. After a couple of hours of playing, our team was down by six in our current game, but we were all laughing and having a good time.

I looked up at the sky, and then shut my eyes, loving the feel of the late afternoon sun on my skin. And then a shadow passed over the court and I blinked. I heard the distinctive tick... tick... tick... coming from above us.

"James!" I called as I stared at the bat like creature diving toward me.

"What in all creation is that?" Finch shouted as he looked around, I hoped for something he could move telekinetically into the creature to hit it away from us.

"I see it!" James said moving toward me. "Pull up

your magic, I'm practically mortal right now," he muttered next to me.

I did as he suggested and pulled up my magic, pulling energy from all around me.

I can't feel anything coming from it, Luci said in my head.

Helen screamed and fainted as the creature swooped over us, its talons extended.

We all ducked low, avoiding it.

"What do we do?" Porta called.

"I got this!" Finch uprooted a tree and when the bat creature got in range, he telekinetically swung the tree like a baseball bat and hit the creature dead center.

The bat crumpled and skidded across the basketball court on its back, hitting the back fencing.

"Score!" Terrance shouted.

"Great hit, Finch!" Quinn crowed.

We cautiously approached the creature, checking to see if it was alive. As we got closer, we noticed a black foggy mist seeping from its eye holes and I was suddenly afraid.

"Everyone back up!" I screamed. "I think it's a Formless One!"

"What?" Quinn frowned.

"Bethany, hit it with your counter-magic, right now," James said urgently.

I nodded and released all the energy magic I'd pulled in at the creature. A white light shot out of my hands, surrounding the creature and we heard a sizzling sound. When the light dissipated, we could see the creature was now covered in a black goo.

"You liquified it!" Finch grinned.

"Porta, Luci, will you check on Helen and get her back inside?" I asked them softly. I feared Helen would avoid me like the plague now.

The girls both nodded and ran back over to Helen.

"What should we do with it?" Quinn asked.

"Should we report this to one of the Professors?" Terrance asked.

"We should take it to Professor Singh," James suggested.

"Think we can get it in the building?"

"Yeah, Bethany and I got the spider in, this guy should be a piece of cake."

"Okay, how do you want to do this?" Finch asked.

I stood there, feeling like I was in a strange daydream. Not moving, just standing there observing. I heard Helen crying behind me, but I didn't turn around until I heard them enter the building. Then I saw someone coming toward us and I blinked, moving toward James, terrified it was whoever was trying to attack me. I breathed a sigh of relief when I realized it was Consuela.

"What is that thing?" she asked looking at the mess in front of us. "Helen was carrying on about a giant bat, but surely that disgusting lump isn't it?"

"It is. It's an automaton."

"Really?" she asked, her eyes brightening. "How does it work?"

"We're not sure. We need to take it to Professor Singh."

"Can I come?"

"Yeah, if you help us carry it," James said with a chuckle.

"Sure. No problem."

I then recalled that since the automaton was mechanical, Consuela would definitely be interested. She was a techno-witch and could hack just about anything. "Maybe you can help Professor Singh figure out how they work."

"I would love to, do you think she'd let me?" she asked, excited at the prospect.

I shrugged. "I don't know. Ask her when we get there."

The boys all squatted down and grabbed corners of the shriveled wings.

"If you two will get the doors, we'll get this inside," James suggested.

We nodded and hurried ahead of them, pulling the doors open. Glancing into the hall, I could see that it was clear. "Okay, we should be able to get to the lab pretty quickly," I commented as James passed me.

Consuela and I scouted ahead, planning to clear the way, if it was needed, but the halls were fairly deserted, thankfully. We made it to the lab in record time. The boys set the creature down on an empty lab table. "We'll get the professor," I said as they all went to the lab sinks to wash their hands.

Consuela and I went next door and knocked.

"Miss Welch, Miss Hernandez, what can I do for you?" Professor Singh looked between us.

"We have another automaton, Professor. A bat-like creature."

"You went outside?" she asked, clearly surprised. "Miss Welch, I imagined you to be smarter than that."

I dropped my head to my chest. "I'm sorry. I wasn't alone, though, and you did say if I was with people I could. James and the others were all with me. We thought it would be okay if there were a group of us."

"Obviously it we were wrong. I think I might have to insist that you stay within the building now."

I sighed. "Yes, Professor."

"Well, show me this creature you've discovered. We'll see what it's all about then."

Consuela and I followed her back to the lab.

"Boys. Thank you for carrying the creature in. I think you can all leave now, I can handle it from here."

"But Professor, we wanted to stay and see what you think of it," Finch insisted.

Professor Singh sighed. "Very well, let me take a look." She pulled a pair of clear glasses from her pocket. "Bethany get everyone glasses."

"Yes, Professor." I went to the drawer and handed out glasses all around.

We all moved to the table next to her. She was quiet as she studied it and then she frowned.

"How did it get covered in this... Black goo?"

"That was, well..." Finch started.

"It was me. Sort of," I admitted. "You see, Finch hit it, knocking it down and then as we moved closer to make sure it was dead, I noticed a Formless One attempting to leave it. James told me to use my magic, so I released this white light, I'm still not sure how I did that, and when the light was gone there was this goo."

"Hmmm."

"We think she liquified it," Finch put in.

Professor Singh nodded. "I think I concur with

your assessment." She walked around the creature, looking it over. "Definitely in the same style as the spiders. I imagine it is the same perpetrator. I'll know more once I dissect it."

"Professor, would it be possible for me to help?" Consuela asked, looking hopeful.

"I suppose that is not a bad idea, Miss Hernandez," Professor Singh said after a moment. "As for the rest of you, I think it is now time for you to return to your weekend activities."

"Yes, Professor," Finch, Quinn and Terrance replied all together. They took off their glasses and dropped them in the container on the shelf by the door.

"Mr. Barret, please see to it that Miss Welch is occupied for the remainder of the weekend in the building, would you? No more adventures out to the courtyards. I'm losing table space with each of these creatures you bring me. Soon I'll have to move to an offsite lab, and I can tell you I do not look forward to that." Professor Singh smiled and I knew she was teasing a bit, though serious about me staying inside the building.

"Yes, Professor, I will," James replied, taking my hand.

As we left, I head the Professor say, "Well, Miss Hernandez, shall we get started?"

The door closed and I dropped my head on James' shoulder and sighed.

"Well that was fun."

He chuckled as we walked. "Dinner?" he asked.

I nodded and we swung by the cafeteria. I ate my chicken salad sandwich and chips in relative silence as he patiently waited for me. Once I was done, he emptied my tray.

"Wait here one minute, okay?"

I nodded and watched as he re-entered the kitchen area. When he returned he was carrying an orange, a bag of cookies and a couple bottles of water. I smiled, he seemed to always know when to plan ahead.

"For later?" I asked, grinning.

"Yep." He shuffled everything into one arm and then took my hand.

We headed back to my room and settled in. James picked up *Chambers of Secrets* and finished reading to the end. As he put it back on my shelf two hours later, he asked, "Do you want to start the next?"

"Sure." I smiled. I loved listening to him read.

CHAPTER 16

JAMES

The next morning, I moved from Bethany's side, letting her sleep a little longer. I picked up my clothes and hurried to the next hall to the boys' bathroom and used the facilities and changed. I head back to her room, hoping that she hadn't woken while I was gone.

Opening her door, I heard her moving around on the bed and quickly moved into the room and closed the door as silently as I could. I set my clothes down on her desk.

"James?" she murmured.

"Good morning, sleeping beauty." I smiled at her as she blinked sleepily at me.

"Morning." She sat up and pushed the covers off of her.

She stretched her arms over her head and then

ran her fingers through her dark wavy hair. She looked like an adorable mess. How anyone could want to rid the world of her was beyond me and I was determined to keep her safe.

"Are you hungry?" I asked, grinning at her.

"Yeah, but I want a shower and stuff first."

"Okay."

I walked with her down to the girls' bathrooms and took up my post outside the door. "I'll be right here."

She blinked her chocolate brown eyes at me and smiled. "Okay."

As I waited, I planned what I was going to do today. I needed to see the Librarian again. I had questions about the automata and the book they had given me. I frowned realizing I hadn't really gotten a chance to read much of it.

"Hey, James," Porta said as she approached the bathroom. "Waiting on Bethany?"

I gave her a half smile. "Yeah, we're gonna head down to the cafeteria, have you eaten?"

Porta nodded. "Yeah, Luci, Helen and I just came from there. Um... how's Bethany doing? She okay?" Porta fidgeted.

"Yeah, she's fine. Worried, but fine."

"Ugh, I don't blame her. I can't believe some jerk

is targeting her after what she went through last year."

I nodded. "Yeah, but we'll figure it out. If you wouldn't mind, we're still hoping to keep it quiet about this jerk and what he's doing to her."

Porta smiled. "Of course." Her smile faded and she looked up at me. "Helen is pretty weirded out. I don't think she'll say anything, but she's... well she's terrified to go back to the room with Bethany. Think she'd mind if I go in and get the rest of Helen's things?"

"I'm sure it's fine. It's not locked, but—" I stopped and looked around to make sure we were alone. Dropping my voice I continued softly, "Professor Singh warded the room, so you'd better have good intentions going into her space."

Porta raised her brows. "Of course I do, and I'm glad she did. I imagine that is also being kept quiet?"

I bobbed my head 'yes'.

Porta sighed and her cheek raised as she gave me a half smile. "Okay, if there is anything else I can do, let me know." She pushed open the bathroom door.

"I will." I nodded as she stepped in and let the door close behind her. I continued to worry about Bethany. More specifically about what she would do when I couldn't stay with her at night. I doubted very much that the professors would allow me to continue staying in her room past the holiday.

As the door pulled open, I pushed off the wall and smiled at her. "Ready?"

"Yes, I'm starving."

She gripped my hand and we walked down the hall toward the stairs that would take us down to the dining hall. Once we were there, she picked out a stack of pancakes, grabbed a pitcher of syrup and a tall glass of milk. We settled at a table in the middle of the crowd who were still dining. I was glad to have so many people around, as there was safety in numbers.

"I'll be right back, will you be alright?" I asked her, studying her face for hints of panic.

"I'll be fine." She smiled at me and took a bite.

"Okay, I'll be back." I kissed her cheek and ran my fingers over the opposite one, smiling at her.

I headed out of the cafeteria and over to the nurse for a bite to eat myself. It didn't take longer than fifteen minutes and once I'd finished I hurried back to her. She'd finished eating, but was sitting quietly and nursing her milk, taking tiny sips as she waited for me. Seeing me, she downed the rest of the glass and then smiled.

I grinned at her. "So what is on our agenda

today?" I asked, wondering what she was going to do today.

"I don't know. I... well I don't want to be alone." She looked down shyly. "I actually thought I might go see if I can talk to Professor Ubel. I want to see if he'll work with me again."

I considered her words, it was a good idea, if he'd be willing to train her some more. "Okay, It's a Sunday, but he should be in his office for a little while this morning." I knew all of the professors kept office ours in the mornings on the weekends, just in case a student needed something official. There were others who were available in the afternoons, but it was random which ones would be on duty. "I have some things I need to take care of. Can we meet up later?" I held her hands and squeezed her fingers gently in mine.

"Sure. You'll text me or come find me?"

"I will," I assured her.

"Okay, see you later." She leaned forward and kissed my lips softly, tasting of maple syrup and milk.

We parted ways and I went down to the library, running into Lukas who was monitoring the halls. I sighed as he stood, blocking my way with his muscled arms crossed over his massive chest. The guy was a red-headed Russian Hulk and could probably break me in two with just a thought.

"What are you doing down here, Strigoi? I know I've told you before, this is the Academy Library, not your personal browsing facility," Lukas snarled gruffly.

"Good morning to you too, Lukas." I tried for friendly. "I merely wished to speak to the Librarian about a book they gave me—"

"And do you have appointment?" Lukas arched a brow at me.

"Well, no, but—"

"You come back when you have an appointment or a pass from a Professor." Lukas smirked at me.

I started to turn around when the Librarian appeared and brushed a hand against Lukas' arm. He looked down and frowned at the Librarian.

"Are you sure?" Lukas asked, arching a brow.

The Librarian's lip raised in a half smile and they blinked.

"Very well, Strigoi. The Librarian has granted you a pass."

I ducked under Lukas' arm and into the library. "Thank you for seeing me."

The Librarian inclined the head in a nod of acknowledgement and then gestured to a chair.

I took the seat as directed and they took the seat opposite of me, staring at me intently. I squirmed beneath their gaze.

"Um... I wanted to asked about the book—"

The book suddenly appeared in the Librarian's hand and they held it out to me again.

"Yes, this book. I, ah, I haven't gotten through it all the way, but I wanted to know if the automata could be used, like possessed—"

Taking the book from me, the Librarian opened the book about a third of the way in, gestured to the chapter, and then handed it back to me with a smile.

I pulled the book closer and read, "Automata are created mostly as vessels for entities or magical forces by those who practice the dark arts." I looked up at the Librarian and said, "So they can be possessed by Formless Ones?"

The Librarian gave me a single nod.

"Does a dark witch have to be the one to create the Automata?" I frowned. "I mean, can a Formless One or a Black Annis create them on their own, or do they need help?"

The Librarian smiled and held up a single finger.

"What?" I asked confused and then I realized. "Oh, one question at a time. Right. So, can a Formless One or Black Annis create an automaton?"

The Librarian shook their head no.

"So a dark witch—"

The Librarian gave me a look that said it was possibly a dark witch, but didn't have to be a witch necessarily, so I asked, just to be sure.

"Or someone of our supernatural world practicing the dark arts created the automatons?"

Nodding, the Librarian smiled.

"Are the automata ever used for positive energy?" I asked curiously.

Holding up their hands palms up, the Librarian couldn't say either way with the way I posed my question.

"It is possible to use them for good though?"

The Librarian nodded, yes.

"The automatons that attacked us were not friendly though, right?"

The Librarian rolled their eyes and shook their head no.

"Okay, just checking." I sighed. "May I keep the book a bit longer?"

Nodding yes, the Librarian stood.

I gripped the book and said, "Thank you for helping me."

Smiling the Librarian walked me to the door.

I waved over my shoulder as I moved back into the hallway, running into Lukas' back. "Dude, why are you blocking the door?"

"No one goes in." Lukas grunted.

"I'm coming out, not going in." I pushed past him and shook my head. I was feeling drained from dealing with the nonverbal Librarian and the gruff manner of Lukas. "You know you don't have to be such an ass all the time, Lukas."

Lukas smirked and moved back in front of the door. "Be on your way, Strigoi."

Sighing, I went off to find Bethany as I'd said I would. I had things to tell her anyway.

CHAPTER 17
BETHANY

I sat self-consciously sipping on my glass of milk waiting for James to get finished in the nursing station. I could feel eyes on me and it made me feel weird. I really didn't want to be alone any longer than I had to be. I had been so excited to start this school year and now... now I was afraid it was going to be more like last year than I wanted it to be.

Catching sight of James, I downed the rest of my milk. Without a word, he took the glass from me, and picked up the tray, disposing of them. When he returned, he asked, "So what is on our agenda today?"

I shrugged. "I don't know. I... well I don't want to be alone." I looked down, feeling more eyes on me. I hated this feeling and I wanted to do something about it. I wanted to learn more about how my powers worked. That made me think of something I could do. "I actually thought I might go see if I can talk to Professor Ubel. I want to see if he'll work with me again."

James didn't say anything for a moment. He just sort of studied me, as if trying to figure out what was going on in my head. "Okay, It's a Sunday, but he should be in his office for a little while this morning." He paused for a moment, I guessed he was deciding what he was going to do. "I have some things I need to take care of. Can we meet up later?" He held my hands and squeezed my fingers gently in his, and I knew he was trying to reassure me.

"Sure. You'll text me or come find me?" I said brightly, not wanting him to worry.

"I will." He nodded and smiled at me in that tender way that he had, which made me feel warm and fuzzy.

"Okay, see you later." I leaned forward and kissed his soft but strong lips.

He crossed the cafeteria while I went down the hall that led to the professors' offices. A few minutes later, I stood hesitantly outside of Professor Ubel's office. He was a tall man, and very nice looking, and I had quite the crush on him. Last year he'd given me lessons on counter magic and I really hoped he'd be willing to do so again this year. I was sad that I didn't have any classes with him this year. Once I had my breathing under control, I knocked on the door.

After a minute, the door opened. "Miss Bethany, to what do I owe the pleasure?" Professor Ubel said, as he opened the door wider.

"Hello, Professor, do you have a moment?"

"For you, my dear girl, any time. Come in." He gestured to the chairs in front of his desk.

I entered and took one of the offered chairs and waited for Professor Ubel to return to his own seat. "Thank you."

"Now, what can I do for you, my dear girl?" He folded his hands together on his desk. "Are your classes going well?"

"Oh, yes, they are fine."

"Good, good. How are you liking that new professor you have for History of the Magical World? Chalcamony, is it?"

I smiled. "Professor Chalcedony, I think you mean. He's... well, he takes some getting used to. He... um... he seems to not like the Strigoi in the class very much, Professor."

"Really? Hmmm. I wonder why he's chosen to teach at Dusk Academy then?" Professor Ubel looked deep in thought for a moment. "Well, we'll save that for another discussion, as I don't imagine he is why you are here?"

"No, Professor, that's not why I'm here." I smiled. Biting my lip, I decided to just dive into what I wanted. "Professor, I, well I was hoping you would be willing to work with me again?" I beseeched him, giving him a pleading look. "I have so far been able to do a few defensive things, like we worked on last year, and I was able to create this white light that was pretty powerful, but I have no idea how I did it and, well... I really need to learn more control." I bit my lip again to keep myself from begging further.

Professor Ubel gave me a bemused look and asked, "What brought this on, my dear? Why the sudden interest in learning more now? And when did you manage to create this white light?"

He seemed curious, but somehow anxious to know my answer and I had to consider my words carefully. I trusted him, but something about his questions bothered me and though I was tempted to tell him everything, I held back, merely saying, "Well, you heard about the attack in town a few weeks ago?"

"I did indeed, I imagine it has been the talk of the school." He smiled.

I nodded. I'd known that it was probably all over school by now. "Well, when that Jiangshi attacked at the bistro, I was there with my parents. It attacked a woman right in front of all of us. My parents were worried and hurried into the bistro, but I wanted to stop it from hurting anyone else, so I stayed outside. I had to defend myself, but I wasn't sure I would be able to stop it. I don't trust my control enough yet. I was lucky that Professor Singh and the Dusk Knights arrived when they did."

"It was indeed *fortunate* that they arrived just in time to help." His lips rose a fraction higher, but it didn't quite reach his eyes.

I nodded. "It was. I was very grateful they arrived at that moment. Anyway, I want to learn more about my powers and how to control them. And the only way for me to gain control and learn is from someone like you, Professor. You and I have similar powers and last year you were so helpful to me. I enjoyed learning from you." I smiled, hoping he would agree.

"Well, I am very busy this semester, my dear girl, so I will have to contemplate your request and see if I can find the time to accommodate you."

Feeling a bit frustrated, I gave him a small smile and nodded. "I understand, Professor. Thank you." I stood up and moved around my chair.

"Bethany, I am pleased that you came to me." He stood as well and walked around his desk, reaching for my arm. "I will let you know my answer soon."

His hand on my arm gave me a weird feeling and I suddenly felt slightly uncomfortable, but I couldn't figure out why. I'd spent plenty of time alone with him over the last year and never felt like that. I mentally shook my head, dismissing my thoughts as merely paranoia over everything that had already happened this year. "Thank you, Professor," I commented again, giving him a real smile as he opened the door.

"My door is always open to you, my dear girl." He looked at me kindly, and gave me a pleasant smile.

I nodded and went out into the hallway. "Goodbye, Professor," I murmured, happy that I hadn't given in to the paranoia and run from him. I just wished that he'd given me a definitive answer about working with me. I didn't know what I would do if he said no.

I trudged down the deserted hallway, looking down at my feet. I was in my own little world, so when I heard his door shut with a loud click, I jumped a little. Being on my own was making me a lot more paranoid than any person should be. I wanted to be around people where I felt safer, even if they were whispering about me, so I returned to the dining hall. It was nearing lunch time, but I wasn't really hungry having eaten all those pancakes a little over an hour earlier.

As I sat down, my phone rang. My first thought was that it was James, but then I realized it couldn't have been him. It was my mom's ring tone and I wondered why she was calling. I had only been gone three months. Last year she'd only called me at Thanksgiving and Christmas time. It was very unlike her to call me randomly in the middle of the year for no reason. Maybe I'd forgotten something at home? I stared at my phone for a moment trying to figure out why she was calling and then realized I'd better answer or she would get mad at me and do something drastic, like cancel my phone account. I couldn't allow that. I had to have my phone. What teenage girl could live without one?

CHAPTER 18
BETHANY

Frowning I answered, "Mom is everything okay?"

"Bethany," a voice sounding almost like my mother's hissed my name.

That was weird, I thought. *Maybe I am mistaken and it isn't her?* I pulled my phone from my ear and looked at the screen. It simply said 'Mom's calling' and showed her picture... *It's her number...* I thought, and then shivered as I recalled that dream... it had said the same thing on my phone screen in the dream. And I knew that was wrong. My phone should have only said 'Mom' and shown the number, but there was no number showing. Half afraid, I put the phone back to my ear. "Mom," I said hesitantly, "I think there's something wrong with my phone. You sound funny, is everything okay? It's not Dad is it?"

"Bethany," the voice hissed again, "you're still seeing that disgusting vile creature!"

My eyes widened and I looked around the dining hall. It was full of other students, both witches and vampires, sitting together loudly talking and eating, well the witches were eating, but no one seemed to be paying special attention to me. I stood on the edge of the dining hall, looking out over all the tables and couldn't find anyone who was on their phone and appeared to be insane. Just a bunch of mostly normal teens enjoying their Saturday with their friends.

I started trembling, but I had to find out who was doing this to me. "Who is this?" My voice shook with fear. *This can't be my mother,* I thought, *I know it isn't Mom, it's got to be whoever is after me.* I knew there was no way for my mom to know I was still seeing James, and no one even knew she didn't want me seeing him, well except for Helen, but it wasn't as if she were gonna go calling my mom and tattle on me, no matter how upset she was about the automata. No, whoever this was, it wasn't my mother. Whoever this was sounded deranged and evil. Victoria popped into my head, but it didn't sound like her either, besides the fact that she'd disappeared last year and no one had seen or heard from her since the Formless One had taken her away.

"You stupid child, I told you, I told you not to see

that abominable creature! I told you not to defile yourself by being with something like him! You are a disobedient petulant abhorrent girl!" The voice on the phone, still sounding vaguely like my mother, distorted horribly and sounded more demonic and terrifying.

Definitely not my mother or Victoria! I shook and tears started streaming down my face. My throat closed in terror and I couldn't speak. Who would be so cruel? Why were they doing this to me? What had I done to deserve to be spoken to in such a way?

"Nasty, despicable girl, you'll get what's coming to you," the voice mocked. "We are watching, we are coming, you will pay for your crimes against nature, you repulsive, disgusting unnatural child!"

Without realizing it, my magic began to react with my phone, and it began to sizzle in my hand as my magic flowed into the device. It crackled and sizzled, a bright white light shone from the screen and then the distorting voice and its hurtful words dissolved into inaudible nonsense. Black mist started to rise from the phone, but the magical white light charge I was somehow putting off enveloped the mist and crushed it back into the casing of the phone, causing it to get hot and bubble in my hand.

My eyes widened even bigger as I stood there shaking and staring at my now useless phone. It was as if I was invisible, no one noticed my distress. No one came over to see what was wrong with me. No one offered help of any kind. They just continued chatting and eating as if I didn't even exist. This frightened me even more, making my heart race as I panicked.

I couldn't move. My feet felt as though I was glued in place. Stuck for eternity, unable to speak. Unable to move. Never to be seen. Fear filled every inch of my being as people walked by me, oblivious to the terror I was experiencing even though they were less than a foot from me.

Finally, after several long, tortuous minutes, I was able to move my fingers and I dropped my phone with a loud clatter. It bounced several times and disappeared behind a column with a potted plant. My vocal cords loosened and I screamed long and loud, releasing all of the panic and terror I felt into the scream. Able to move my feet again, I began to run. I had to get away. Away from the room. Away from the people. But most especially, away from my phone!

CHAPTER 19
BETHANY

Just wanting to get away, I ran for the nearest exit. I couldn't stand it. I had to be away from there immediately. My fear drove me to push open the outer doors of the Academy, despite being safer behind their wards, and out into the courtyard. I moved with a speed that would have wowed any marathon runner. I ran as if the hounds of hell were nipping at my heels and would gobble me up if I stopped. It was the type of blind panic that drove people to do stupid things and I was acting like the Queen of Stupid by racing from the perceived danger I'd felt holding my phone in the dining hall straight into the arms of the waiting enemy!

Luckily, I came to my senses and stopped suddenly before actually slamming myself into a giant web. Literally. A spun web reached from the side of the clock tower to the neighboring copse of trees. I heard that terrifying tick, tick, tick, tick, that told me spiders and possibly other automata were close. And as if that thought conjured them, a whole pack of spiders dropped from the trees and a group of the bats swooped down from the top of the clock tower to encircle me and herd me closer toward the web.

I spun in a circle as they moved toward me, hissing, and ticking louder and louder. The bats reached down at me with their taloned feet. I ducked and then closed my eyes and prayed. Carefully I began pulling in energy, hoping beyond hope that I could blast one of the spiders out of the way and get away, but I knew it was a feeble plan. The bats could swoop in and grab me as I ran. Opening my eyes, I turned slowly in a circle, planning to look for the weakest or smallest spider only to find another giant creature in front of me.

I screamed, taking in its bizarre appearance. It looked somewhat like a greyhound only more muscular, bred with a razorback, and maybe a ram with long curled horns on its head. Its back was to me and its long tail, much longer than a dog's tail, was whipping around smacking spiders back away from me, from us. When I screamed, it turned its head toward me, its jaws opening showing off sharp jagged teeth and a pair of fangs that came down past its lower jaw like a sabretooth tiger. Drool dripped from the lower jaw, and it snarled, whipping the tail toward me, but missing and I heard a distinct hiss and crunch from behind me.

I looked over my shoulder to see a crumpled bat. The creature's tail had hit it, killing it. Its tail whipped again and hit at a spider, blasting it into the one next to it, taking them out of my path back to the school. I was thankful to now have a path out of the circle of spiders, but I worried about the bats as I turned and took off back toward the building.

The creature, seeing me move raced after me, its tail lashing out to the sides. Out of the corner of my eye, I saw the creature rear back on its powerful hind legs and launch itself in the air. I screamed again, as it came down next to me, a giant bat crushed in its massive jaws.

I suddenly realized the creature, whatever it was, wasn't an automaton and was trying to help me, to protect me. I connected with its dark gaze, its huge set eyes stared at me, but didn't seem to hold any malice toward me. They instead looked almost *kind*. It spun again, and swiped at a spider, shredding it with its massive claws as it bit into and snapped another in half.

I moved slowly backwards toward the building, keeping my eyes on the sky, watching for bats. I headed, I hoped toward the stairs that led up to the glass hallway doors of the Academy. The creature continued to attack the spiders and bats as they attempted to reach me. Finally, my back hit the door and I paused, watching the battle before me. I wondered where the creature had come from and why it was protecting me.

After it killed another couple of spiders and the last bat that I could see, they began to retreat, scurrying back toward the trees, to the giant web they'd created. The courtyard was littered with multiple automata bodies. The creature stood before me with its back to me, watching the spiders retreat also. It stayed where it was for another few minutes, as if guarding me, and then it turned its head toward me and raised its chin at me sharply.

Somehow, I knew it was telling me to go in the building, and as I opened the door, it raced off toward the end of the main building and around the corner, out of sight. Once inside, I leaned back against the closed door and attempted to catch my breath. As I looked up, I saw James and several of our vampire friends hurrying toward me.

CHAPTER 20

JAMES

I figured I'd better drop the automata book off in my room before going to find Bethany, so that was my first stop. It was heavy and I didn't want anything to happen to it. I knew it was a rare book and I had to be careful with it. I tried calling Bethany, but her phone just went straight to voicemail which was weird.

I frowned as I set the book down on my desk. Bethany always kept her phone charged. It never went straight to voicemail, so I was a bit concerned, especially since I knew for a fact that it had charged the night before while I was reading *Harry Potter and the Prisoner of Azkaban* to her. There was no way it could have died already. And I doubted that she would turn it off, not knowing that I was going to text her.

"What's up, man?" Cory asked, seeing the look on my face.

I held up my phone. "Trying to call Bethany, but it keeps going to voicemail."

"So? Maybe she forgot to charge it, or turned it off for something. Maybe she's watching a movie and doesn't want to be interrupted. It's not a world ending occurrence, man." Cory shook his head at me.

I supposed she could have turned it off while she met with Professor Ubel. "Maybe. She did say she was going to go talk to Professor Ubel and see if he'd train her some more." I frowned.

"See? Nothing to get your panties in a wad over. She'll call when she's done, I'm sure."

"Yeah, maybe." Still, I worried. Something felt... *off*.

I turned toward the door. I figured that I could go up to the dining room, maybe take a walk by Professor Ubel's office, see if I could figure out where she was. Maybe one of her friends had seen her. "I'll be back later."

Cory smirked. "Man, you are so whipped." He chuckled as I started to pull the door shut behind me.

"Cors, with everything going on, I'm just worried, okay?" I frowned at him.

"Not everything is out to get her. And she's a brave one, I am sure she's fine, man."

I shook my head, ignoring him, I hadn't told him about everything, and I had a gut feeling something was wrong. When it came to her, I trusted my instincts over Cory. I went up to the dining hall. There were a lot of people about talking loudly and laughing. I paid little attention to them until I over-heard Bethany's name. I spun around to pinpoint the voice and then, seeing two young male witches, I turned toward them and listened, moving closer, so I wouldn't miss what they were saying.

"Dude, it was so bizarre. She was just standing there and then started screaming."

"What? Like at someone?" the smaller of the boys said, looking confused.

"No, like she was in the middle of a horror movie, dude. I mean she could give the scream queens a run for their money!" He laughed.

I wanted to crush his wind pipe, but I restrained myself. I had to know more of what happened. Why had she been screaming? It didn't make any sense.

"Crazy. Where'd she go?"

Balling my hands into fists, I paid special atten-tion to the male witch's answer. "Who knows? I mean she threw her phone down over there and it bounced like six times and she just ran that way." He was still chuckling.

It was an irritating and grating sound that I wanted to pound out of him.

"Dude, did you go get the phone? I mean she might have some nice pics on there."

I snarled and before I could stop myself, I grabbed the small male witch who'd made the suggestion by the front of his shirt. "Don't even think about her that way!"

The other witch raised his hands in defense. "Geez, sorry, dude, didn't know she was off limits!"

"Yeah, sorry! I didn't mean anything by it!" the one in my hands agreed, a look of fright on his face.

I shoved him away, breathing hard. I looked at the witch who'd been telling what happened to her. "Where. Is. Her. Phone?" I stared at him, not bothering to remove the look of hatred from my face. If she was injured, I was going to come back and give these two a real fright. *How dare they not help her!*

He looked at me, shaking and panicked. He pointed to behind a potted plant. "I-it's st-stilllll th-there, d-dude," he stuttered.

I gave him a nod and he and his buddy took off. I went over to the plant, shoving it out of the way, and picked up her phone. I could tell it was completely fried, the screen cracked into a billion pieces and the back melted into a black gooey mess. I knew in my gut how it had become such a mess. I had an idea of what had to have caused her to use her counter magic on her phone, but how a Formless One had gotten into it, I had no clue. This was bad. *Damn*. I ran my hand through my hair feeling terror in my heart.

I'd promised her I would keep her safe, and now she was missing.

With shaking fingers, I pulled out my phone and called Cory. Every second he took to answer was like a knife stab in my heart.

"Find her?" he snorted into the phone, his voice filled with mirth.

"No, something's wrong. I found her phone in the cafeteria. It's a melted black mess. She's fried it and everyone in here is talking about how she freaked out and took off. Cory, I'm worried. I have to find her." I knew he could hear the panic and terror in my voice.

"Man." Cory sounded suddenly serious. "You want me to get some of the others and help look?" he offered.

"Yeah, would you?" I said gratefully.

"I'm on it, man, we'll find her."

I'D ALREADY SEARCHED THE PROFESSORS' HALLWAY,

and I was making my way through the maze of witch hallways asking if anyone had seen her, but so far, I was out of luck. My gut told me she wasn't up here, but I didn't know where else to look. I hoped she hadn't gone outside, if she had, she would be more vulnerable to attack.

"Hey, have you seen Bethany?" I asked a tall Asian girl, I thought her name was Martha, but I wasn't positive.

"Sorry, no. I haven't seen her." She shook her head, her long, dark hair flowing around her shoulders as she did.

"Okay, if you do, could you tell her I'm looking for her?" I asked.

"Yeah, sure," she replied with a nod.

As I turned to go down another hall, my phone rang.

"Yeah?" I answered, seeing it was Cory.

"I see her, you're gonna wanna get here, like now, man," Cory said.

"Where?"

"West doors, she's outside."

"What?" I muttered feeling my heart begin a panicked beating in my chest. "I'll be there in a second."

Why did she go outside? I thought as I shut off my

phone and then raced back down the hall I was in. I tore through three more hallways and down two flights of stairs and then down another two hallways. I slammed into my friends who were blocking the hall from use.

"What the hell, man?" I asked seeing them all standing there.

"Something's going on out there..." Cory pointed at the door where I could see Bethany standing with her back pressed to the glass.

I shoved him out of the way and started down the hall toward her as she opened the door and slipped inside. She leaned against the door and bent over, panting. I moved closer and she looked up.

"Bethany!" I hurried toward her with our friends right on my heels.

When I reached her, I pulled her into a hug and held her close. She wrapped herself around me and sobbed for a minute. Our friends surrounded us doing their best to keep us hidden from anyone else who was in the hall or walking by.

"What happened? I thought you were going to see Professor Ubel."

She nodded and said, "I did." It was muffled against my chest, but I easily understood her. She took a calming breath and explained, "I went back to the cafeteria after and I got this weird phone call. I thought it was Mom at first, but it wasn't. Something evil, demonic... it was awful."

"Is that why your phone looks like this?" I held up the destroyed device.

Bethany pushed away from my chest and backed away from me, well from it. Her eyes widened and took on a look of horror. She began to shake and I knew she was drawing in energy, getting ready to blast the device again.

Before she could, I handed it off to Tran. "Do something with this."

He took it from me with two fingers. "Get rid of it?" he asked.

"No, get it to Professor Singh, if you can."

He nodded and took off down the hall with his brother Kale and sister Fira.

With the device gone, Bethany seemed to come back into herself and stepped back into my arms. "Thank you," she murmured.

I wrapped myself around her protectively. "Why did you go outside? You know it isn't safe out there."

She shook her head. "I know it was stupid. I was panicked and not thinking. I ran into a swarm of spiders and bats and I thought I was going to die." She sniffled and then gave me a watery smile. "Then the strangest thing happened."

Jodie rubbed her back, comforting her. "What happened?" she asked before I could.

"This creature appeared and at first I thought it was after me too, but it started attacking the spiders and bats and it saved me." She looked up from my chest and smiled in wonder.

I let out the breath I'd been holding. "What kind of creature was it?" I asked.

"I don't know. It looked almost hideous, but it had kind eyes."

I looked over at Cory and arched a brow.

"Bethany," Cory said gently, as if he was talking to a skittish animal, "what kind of animal was it closest to?"

She looked over at him and squished up her nose. "A dog maybe? Skinny like a greyhound, sort of, but muscular too. Oh and it had this ridged strip over its back with black hair. I don't know why, but it kind of reminded me of *Pumba,* you know, from *Lion King?* But more defined. And it had thick long fangs that came down past its lower jaw, and horns on its head that curled like a ram's."

Cory nodded looking awed at her words. "Wow. What you're describing... sounds a lot like a chupacabra."

"A what?" Bethany asked, looking at Cory curiously.

"Cory specializes in magical creatures," Jodie explained. "He knows all about different supernatural creatures."

"It's magical?" she asked, sounding less frightened and more curious.

"A chupacabra is intelligent, for an animal. One of the most intelligent on the planet. From what I know of it, it is like a vampire, meaning it feeds on blood, but it avoids humans and generally only feeds on live-stock and other large animals. They are rarely ever seen, which is why they are spoken about so often as myths. I have a book on them back in our room."

"Can we go take a look?" I asked.

"Sure." Cory nodded. "I'm glad you're okay, Bethany." He smiled.

Jodie hugged her, brushing her hair from her face. "I'm glad you're okay too." She kissed Bethany's cheek. "I'm off to go see Terrance, but if you need anything, you come see me, okay? I miss my roomie." She grinned.

Bethany nodded and smiled at her. "Thanks, Jodie, I miss you too."

"We have to have a girls' day soon, okay?" Jodie suggested.

"I'd like that." Bethany grinned and curled back into me.

Most of the others had dispersed after that with,

"Glad you're alright, Bethany," and "Glad you didn't get eaten by the spiders and bats, Bethany," which made her laugh.

"Me too," she murmured, still laughing.

We followed Cory back to our room and waited as he went through his bookshelf looking for the correct book.

"Here we go." He opened the book and read for a minute.

While he read, Bethany and I settled on my bed, with her curled up in my lap and snuggled into my shoulder.

"Okay, well this is interesting." Cory puffed out his cheeks and then blew out a breath. He looked over at me. "So it says the Ancient often uses the chupacabras to protect those they deem worthy. It says that the Ancient has a loyal pack of them and sends them out when needed most."

"The Ancient?" My heart stilled in my chest.

Bethany looked up at me in confusion. "So who is the Ancient person?"

I pressed my lips together, not wanting to answer her.

Cory shrugged and shook his head. "I'm not getting involved, man. Not with the Ancient. You tell her." He shut the book and shoved it back on the shelf. "I'm headed to the commons for some video games. See ya."

I nodded as he left, but still didn't say anything.

"James?" Bethany sat up and looked at me. "James, who is the Ancient person?"

I pressed my lips together and shook my head. Breathing hard, I said, "Let's get you back to your room. It's safer there."

She frowned at me. "But—"

I placed a finger against her lips and then kissed her. "Your room."

Frowning, she gave in and we headed out.

My day's adventure still had me feeling vulnerable, but I hated feeling that way. I wanted to know more about this new world I was now a part of and it seem as if every step forward sent me off into another tangent and I never found out everything I needed to know. How was I supposed to survive if I didn't know how to control my magic? Or what creatures were good or bad? What if I trusted the wrong person? What if I used my magic against a creature thinking it was evil, but like the chupacabra merely looked scary, but was really a protector? All of these 'what ifs' were driving me insane and I really just wanted answers. At the moment though, I really wanted James to tell me about this Ancient person he was being so secretive about.

We were half way to my room when my stomach rumbled. Breakfast seemed as if it had been days ago. "I'm hungry," I commented softly as we walked.

"We'll swing by the dining hall." James turned down a different hallway, taking us on a more direct route to the kitchens.

"Thank you," I murmured. Once we reached the cafeteria line, I grabbed a couple of sandwiches, an apple, a bag of chips and a couple cookies. I looked up at James, daring him to say anything, but he was a smart man and kept his mouth shut.

He took the food from me and carried it as we set back off toward my room. When we reached my dorm room, I checked the wards to be sure they were still active.

"They don't look like they've been disturbed," I murmured as I opened the door.

I didn't see any signs that Helen had come back and that made me sad. I sighed and sat down on my bed. James handed me my food and I unwrapped one of the sandwiches, taking a bite. He sat down next to me, but didn't say anything.

Once I'd eaten half, and he still hadn't said anything, I swallowed and then said, "Spill it. Who is this Ancient person?"

James sighed. "The Ancient is a very powerful being. No one actually knows what the Ancient is, because he has been around longer than all the vampires and witches combined. Everything surrounding the Ancient is secretive and most of us avoid talking about him for fear that in doing so will draw his attention."

"Okay, so he is more powerful than all the supernatural creatures?" I asked trying to imagine what kind of being he was.

"Yes. There are a lot of myths and rumors about the Ancient, but no one knows for sure the full extent of his power. He was actually the driving force between the Vampire and Witch Treaty."

"So, he's good?" I asked, still trying to wrap my head around a being so old and powerful.

"Well, yes and no." James shrugged. "The Ancient is like a force of nature. Benevolent at times and predatory at others. Really it depends on the events taking place." He took my hands in his, rubbing them soothingly. "I think that in your case, he's being benevolent. Sending the chupacabra to protect you was a favorable thing to do, so I don't think you should worry."

I nodded. "Will he continue to be benevolent toward me, do you think?" I queried, biting my lip. "I mean will he continue to send the chupacabra to protect me?"

"Honestly?" James looked at me, frowning. "I

don't know. Maybe. Obviously, there is a reason behind him sending the chupacabra out at that point, he didn't want you harmed. His reason why though, I couldn't tell you. Maybe he needs you for some purpose?"

I don't know why, but that was actually a sort of terrifying thought. An Ancient being who thought I would have some purpose in the future, be it for good or evil, yeah I think I would have rather gone unnoticed by the lot of them. Not knowing what was going on was frightening and I was thankful to have James on my side.

Eating the rest of my sandwich, I snuggled up to him. "Will you stay again tonight?" I asked softly.

James smiled sweetly and pulled me close. "Of course. I'll have to go back to my dorm tomorrow though. Professor Singh said I could stay the weekend, but I doubt the rest of the professors will allow me to stay beyond that, but you are safe here. Professor Singh's wards are powerful. I don't think you will need to worry about being attacked in here again."

I nodded and then sighed. "Thank you."

"Want to finish *Prisoner of Azkaban*?" he asked, picking up the book.

Smiling I nodded against his chest. "Yes, please."

"Where did we leave off?" James asked flipping through the book.

"I think I fell asleep early, like after bus with the shrunken head."

James found the proper page and began to read. His voice was soothing and calming even though the action of the story was rather intense. I finished off the second sandwich and started on the apple as he read about Harry and Ron in divination class. And I realized I had a question about the previous book, relating to real life.

"Hey, I have a question. Kind of weird though."

James chuckled. "What is it?" he said curiously.

"Basilisks, are they real?" I looked at him with wide eyes, half hoping he'd say no.

"What, like the one in *Chamber of Secrets*?"

"Yes, since Cory knows all this stuff, I figured you know, being his best friend, maybe you'd know. So, are they?" I asked, thinking if they were, I never wanted to come into contact with one.

"I don't know, maybe? That really is a question better suited for Cory, he doesn't tell me everything," he replied with a chuckle. "If they are, I imagine they are rare and not as big as the one in *Harry Potter*. I'm pretty sure we would have heard about it by now if they did exist."

"So like bigfoots then," I put in.

"Oh, bigfoots are definitely real," James commented with a laugh.

"What?" My eyes went wide and my jaw dropped.

"Eh, yeah, they're out there, roaming around in woods and mountainous areas. Keep to themselves though, most of the time."

"You're kidding, right?" Narrowing my eyes, I looked at him suspiciously.

"Maybe." He laughed.

"Oh, you!" I pushed against his chest and laughed. I tossed the apple core in the garbage and grabbed the chips before snuggling back against him.

"Comfy?" he asked with a smile.

I grinned. "Yes."

"Okay." He began to read some more and when he finished the book, he immediately picked up the next one, *Goblet of Fire*, and began it.

This time I made it all the way to Harry getting in the prefects' tub with the egg, but my eyes were drooping and my head felt heavy.

"I think you had better get under the covers," James said softly, brushing my hair behind my ear. He picked up the bag of chips and the cookies I hadn't bothered to eat and set them on my desk.

I didn't know if I should change clothes; I knew I didn't want to leave the room. I glanced at him and frowned.

"What?"

"I want to put on my night shirt."

He smiled. "I'll turn around."

I nodded. "Thanks. No peeking."

He chuckled but turned around as I pulled my top over my head, took off my bra and slipped my night shirt on. Then I undid my jeans and pulled them off too. I tossed them in the hamper and then slid beneath my blanket and laid down on my side. "You'll stay?" I murmured.

"I told you I would," he replied with a soft smile.

He laid down next to me and wrapped me in his arms and I fell asleep.

CHAPTER 22

BETHANY

When I woke the next morning, it was Monday, but a holiday, so no classes. James was still with me, awake and reading on his phone. I smiled. Seeing him sitting there, watching over me, made me feel protected. Yawning, I sat up as he set his phone down.

"Good morning, beautiful." He looked a little tired.

I wondered if he'd slept at all, so I asked, "Did you get any sleep?"

"Not really. I figured I would take you down to the dining hall, and then I'd head back over to my dorm and get a bit. Will you be okay?" he asked, concern marring his handsome face.

I did my best to give him a brave smile. "I'll be

okay. I won't go outside and I'll either come back here or be in the commons with a crowd."

He kissed my cheek and slid off the bed. "Why don't you go get changed and then we'll go down?"

"Okay," I agreed. I gathered up fresh clothes and we walked down to the bathroom.

Inside, I set my clothes on a bench and stripped. I turned the water on to hot and stepped beneath the spray. I quickly washed my hair and body and then shut the water off and got out, drying off. I dressed, brushed my wet hair and pulled it back in a ponytail. Pulling out my toothbrush, I brushed my teeth, then gathered up my dirty laundry and left. I'd been gone fifteen minutes and when I stepped back out into the hall, I noticed James was leaning against the wall, his eyes closed.

I walked up to him slowly, and standing on my tip toes, I brushed my lips against his. He cracked a smile and opened his eyes. His arms came around me and he kissed me properly, deepening the kiss and making my insides melt, like he always did.

I shivered at the feeling and smiled as we broke apart. "Mmmm."

"My thoughts exactly." His eyes brightened.

We dropped my stuff back at my room and then headed down to the dining hall. I grabbed a plate of waffles and a chocolate donut and then we went out to the tables. I scanned the room and noticed Finch and Quinn at a table.

"You'll be okay?" James asked hesitantly.

"I'll be fine." I smiled. "I'll go hang out with Finch and Quinn for a bit and then head back to my room, maybe do some homework." I sighed at the thought.

"Then I will see you tomorrow in class," he whispered and kissed my cheek before striding off in the direction of the vampire dorms.

I was a little sad that he was leaving me on my own, but I needed to get used to it. I couldn't have him with me twenty-four-seven, as much as I wished it. Pasting a smile on my lips, I joined Finch and Quinn at their table and joined in their conversation about which *Avenger* superhero was better, *Hawkeye* or *Falcon*. I was all for Hawkeye, along with Quinn, but Finch was siding with Falcon, because of his feathers.

"He flies, that is better than being able to take an accurate shot, and he controls birds," Finch argued.

"His feathers are fake though, anybody could wear them—" Quinn argued.

"And *Hawkeye* is more than just an accurate shot, he can also change his size and mass," I added, thinking about what I knew from the comics.

"Only in the comics, they haven't added that to the movies yet, so you can't count it," Finch disagreed.

Our conversation went on for while, and then when I went to pull my phone out to check some facts, I realized that I didn't have one anymore. "Well shoot," I pouted, feeling completely lost without my mobile device.

"What's wrong, Bethany?" Quinn asked.

"My phone's broken. I forgot."

"Can you get a new one?" Finch asked.

"I don't know, maybe? I'd have to call my parents."

Quinn handed me his phone. "Call them. What's the worst they could say?" he asked shrugging.

Nodding, I took his phone and dialed my dad. He would be a little more reasonable I thought. I waited a moment and then he picked up.

"Hello?"

"Hi, Dad," I commented into the phone brightly.

"Bethany? Why are you calling from this number? Where's your phone?"

"About that, Daddy, that's why I'm calling," I explained. "There was an accident and my phone got destroyed."

"An accident?" Dad sounded confused. "What happened?"

"Well, I was practicing some of my magic and it sort of melted my phone," I lied. It was wrong of me, but if I'd told him what really happened, he'd get in his car and come get me; taking me away from school and put me someplace he deemed safe.

"Bethany," he said, sounding disappointed in me. "You've got to be more careful."

I let out a sound that was halfway between a laugh and a cry. "I know, Dad, I'm sorry."

"Are you okay? You didn't get hurt performing this magic did you?"

I smiled. "I'm fine, Dad. I didn't get hurt. Promise. The thing is, I could really use a new phone..."

Dad sighed. "Alright, I'll see what I can do."

"Thanks, Dad," I said. "How's Mom?" I asked, hoping he wouldn't hand her the phone.

"She's doing fine, she's out shopping with her friend Brenda. Other than the magic mishap are you doing all right?"

"I am. My classes are going, well, most of them anyway are going fine."

"Good, good. Do you need anything else, sweetheart?" Dad asked.

"No, just the phone."

"Okay, I'll take a look and see what I can find and have it sent to you."

"Thanks, Dad."

"You're welcome, sweetheart. Behave, and no more magic with your phone, okay?"

I smiled. "Okay. Promise. Thanks, Daddy."

"Bye, sweetheart."

"Bye!"

When he hung up, I returned the phone to Quinn. "Thanks. My dad's going to send me a new one. Might be a day or two."

Quinn nodded. "Anytime. If you need to borrow it, just ask, I don't mind."

"Thanks, Quinn."

Four Days later

I WAS SITTING IN THE WITCHES' COMMONS AREA with Luci and Porta when Professor Zin approached me with a package. We had been studying for a test in potions, a class we all shared.

"Miss Welch, a package has arrived for you." She handed me the brown box addressed to me.

"Thank you, Professor. I'm sorry you had to deliver it, I would have come to the office to get it."

"I told Vivian I would bring it as I was coming this direction anyway. I knew you were here, I saw you on the monitors." Professor Zin smiled. "Now, if you'll excuse me, I have some tests to grade." She continued through the commons and down the hall.

"What did you get?" Porta asked.

I shook the box and looked at the label. "Oh, it's my new phone. My dad must have found one for me." I smiled and stabbed the box with my pen, slicing through the tape. Opening it, I pulled out a black *Samsung Galaxy 6,* a charging cord and a note from my dad. Unfolding it, I read:

Sweetheart,

After talking to our provider, I was able to get you this phone. It is all ready for you to use and your contacts list and apps have already been reinstalled for you. Jeffery, the IT guy, was able to access your account and retrieve everything you'd backed up to the account, including your pictures. I did not tell your mother about the pictures of you and James on there, as she is still worried about you dating him. We'll leave that topic for another day.

Be careful with this one, as I don't think we can upgrade for another two years now.

Love you, Bethany, be careful with your magic.

Love,

Dad

I refolded the note and pressed the button to open the phone. I put in my old password and sure enough, everything was exactly the same as my previous phone. Over the last several days, I'd had a chance to think about what happened with my old one. I wasn't sure how, but the only thing I could think of was that someone had messed with it. I really needed to go talk to Professor Singh and see if she'd found anything. Gathering up the box and my books, I stood.

"Hey, I need to go see Professor Singh, can we finish this later?" I asked the girls.

Luci nodded. *Go see what she found out about your old phone. And maybe have her ward your new one.*

"Good idea, Luci, I will," I replied, smiling.

"And let us know if you need anything." Porta hugged me. "I know you must be missing Helen, so if you ever want to come stay the night with us, you can."

"Yeah, I don't think she would be too happy about you offering that." I gave her a sad smile. "I think I'm probably better off on my own. Someone seems to be targeting me and I don't want to drag any of you into it," I said softly so I wouldn't be overheard.

We understand. Luci hugged me. *Keep us updated, though, okay?*

I will, I replied telepathically.

With a wave over my shoulder, I headed to Professor Singh's office. On my way out, I tossed the box, but shoved the note in my pocket. Adjusting my books in my arms, I knocked on her door.

"Come in."

Turning the handle, I entered her office. "Hello, Professor." I smiled.

"Bethany, good afternoon. What can I do for you?"

"Uh, well I wondered if you'd found out anything about my phone?"

"Oh, oh yes. Did the Draugr not tell you?" She frowned. "I thought they would have mentioned it."

I shook my head. "I haven't seen the Draugr triplets since my phone broke, we're on different schedules."

"Oh, yes, yes, I imagine you are. Well, as I told them at the time, the phone had been turned into a vessel and it appears that it held one of the Formless Ones, but whatever you did to it, you were able to destroy it as you did with the bat that was possessed. That was the black mass that bubbled on the back of the phone. I'm sorry, I had to drop it in a vat of sulphuric acid to destroy it. You weren't expecting it back, were you?"

"No. No, I definitely wasn't. I had assumed it was the same as the bat too. I just can't figure out..." I stopped talking and took a breath, trying to figure out how to ask her what was bugging me. "Um... how did a Formless One manage to get in my phone, Professor?" I asked.

"Hmmm, that is a very good question. Someone very powerful was able to work the magic on it. The problem is, your magic actually destroyed all traces of the perpetrator's magic, so there is no actual way to tell who might have configured it to be a vessel." She frowned. "So we'll have to come at it from a different angle. Have you left your phone unattended at all? Set it down somewhere and forgot about it? Lost it for any period of time?"

"Not that I can remember. The only time it's not in my possession, is when it's charging in my room, and then during a few of my classes. Just the ones where the professor makes us turn it in as if we're elementary school kids. Not that I mean you, Professor—" I blushed when I realized what I'd said.

Professor Singh grinned and arched a brow at me.

"Anyway," I pushed on, "what I mean to say is my phone sits in the slot with my name on it the whole period during those classes and no one goes near them until the bell rings, so I don't know how—" I shrugged, still blushing over my words.

"You do realize we do it so you all aren't tempted to text during class, and with my class in particular, it is more to save the device from accidental magical interference." Professor Singh grinned. "However, now that I think about it, it could be that the spell was placed on the slot itself, and when you slipped your phone in, it triggered the spell and allowed the Formless One to possess it. Though it would be hard to trace it back to exactly which class now, as the spell trap did its job." The grin faded from her lips and her brow furrowed as she spoke.

"So it could happen again? With another spell trap?" I asked, feeling lost as I stared at her.

"Yes, it could, definitely." She nodded.

"Is there some way to keep that from happening, Professor?" I bit my lip? "Can you ward my phone against that?"

"Yes, I believe we can do something about that. Have you received a new phone yet from your parents?"

I glanced down as I pulled my new phone out of my pocket and nodded. "Yes, my dad just sent it. Can you check it and make sure there hasn't been any magical tampering to it?"

Professor Singh held her hand out for the device. "Yes, that is a good idea." She took the phone from me and turned it on. "Can you put in your password?"

I took the phone back, put in the combination of letters and numbers and then handed it back to her.

She checked every app, every contact and picture in the phone. Then she proceeded to take the back cover off and checked both the battery and the SD card before carefully returning it all to its proper place.

"Is that the charge cord?" she asked looking at the wrapped up wire on top of my books.

I nodded and handed it to her.

She continued examining it. "Alright, it is clean. No magical tampering. I will ward both the phone and the cord, and hopefully it will take care of any further issues. I would recommend coming to me before you download any further applications or adventure onto the web with it. I don't want you taking any chances. And most especially, if anyone sends you an attachment, you have me check it first before opening it. It could contain a basic computer virus, or even some magical virus. If you are uncomfortable bringing it to me, at the very least, take it to Consuela. She will be able to tell, seeing as she's a techno witch." Professor Singh smiled.

"I will, Professor."

"Alright, just give me a few moments and I'll have this all ready for you." Her fingers began to glow and then she transferred the glow to the phone. The glow turned from gold to blue and then green, shimmering over the whole device. And then she picked up the cord again and did the same, transferring the glow to the cord.

"That was neat," I said watching her.

With a smile, she handed it back. "There you go, that should keep out any spell traps, Formless Ones, or anything physical that doesn't belong. I can't do anything about downloads, so you will have to remember what I said about that."

Feeling relieved, I took the phone back from her. "Thank you, Professor."

"My pleasure, my dear. Have you had any other trouble?"

Thinking about it, I said, "No, not since the phone and then me going out in the courtyard and being attacked by spiders and bats again. Since then everything has been pretty calm, thankfully."

"Well, I'm glad the chupacabra was there and you made it back in before they could harm you. You really do need to stay in the building, Bethany. I'll have my knights do another sweep around the campus, but they haven't been able to figure out where the automata are coming from. There have been no breaches of the magical barriers they put up around the campus, so they have to be coming from somewhere within, but you know how large this campus is and the only thing we can figure out is that the perpetrator keeps moving their base of operations."

"I understand. Thank you, Professor." I nodded, looking down at my phone and thinking about what she did to ward it. "Professor?"

"Yes, Bethany?" She looked at me curiously.

"Is there a chance that I could learn how to ward like you do? I know my magic is actually counter-magic, but would it be possible for me to get as good at warding as you?" I asked.

Professor Singh tilted her head, considering my words. I was glad she was taking it as seriously as I meant it when I asked and not just dismissing me. "Yes, I do think it is possible for you to become as good at wards as you are at just about any other type of magic. Just because it is my specialty doesn't mean it can't be one of yours as well. If fact I think it is a very good idea for you to learn it. After all warding is, in its own way, counter-magic. I think it would be very complimentary to your magic."

I smiled, considering her words. "You've been teaching us minor wards in class, when will we move to the more advanced ones?"

"That will have to wait until you are an upper class student, so probably midway through your junior year, I think. It is important for you all to master the simple wards before you move to more complex uses of magic. Right now you are learning the building blocks and it does take time to master them."

I nodded. She'd said the almost the same thing in class, that the wards we were currently learning were the building blocks to more complex spells. "I know, I'm just anxious to be able to do more." I smile ruefully.

"I understand. You are in a unique situation compared to most of the others in class. On top of having more magic in your blood than any of the other students, you are also less trained than them, having grown up with mortal parents. I know that must make things more difficult, but you will get the hang of it. And you did receive additional training from Professor Ubel last year, I'm sure that had to help too."

"It did. He's been very good about helping me. I've asked him if he would continue to train me more. He's busier this year, though, so I don't know if he'll have time."

"I'm sure he will make time for you if he can." Professor Singh smiled.

I sighed. "Well, I suppose I should go now, I still have to study some more for potions. We have an exam tomorrow."

Professor Singh nodded. "Yes, you probably

should get back to studying, potions is not a class you want to make mistakes in." She grinned. "I will see you in class tomorrow, Bethany."

"Thank you again, Professor." I waved at her as I walked out of her office. Feeling much more positive, I headed back to my room.

CHAPTER 23
BETHANY

several weeks passed quickly and I was starting to almost feel normal again. No more run-ins with spiders, bats or any other creepy crawlies. I continued to stay inside, I didn't want to chance running into spiders out in the courtyard, or worse bats dropping down on my head from the sky, and it seemed no one else had any problems with them when they were out on the campus.

Professor Singh had, as she'd said she would, sent the Dusk Knights over to the clock tower to take care of the giant web and the spiders that were still hanging around there. They found a couple of the bats in the tower roof, and cleared them out, but they had not found where they were originating from and they still had no idea who had created them or how they were managing to remain undetected on campus. And no one had reported seeing them or even the chupacabras anymore.

Everyone seemed to be back to being friendly to me, not that my friends had stopped being friendly, but the rest of our classmates had been avoiding me for a while when they heard about the bat incident and then my freakout over the phone. It had been a little hurtful, and I'd worried about it for a short time, but James always cheered me up.

Professor Ubel had finally agreed to tutor me on my magic after classes two days a week, so between working with him and spending time with friends and studying, I'd fallen into a rather normal routine and I was much happier.

"Are you going to see Professor Ubel today?" James asked as we left Professor Chalcedony's class.

I nodded. "Yes, he's showing me more defensive magic. I wish he'd hurry up and show me something to be more proactive rather than reactive. I don't want to have to wait to be attacked by those spiders or bats again."

"Have you told him yet about the white light you created that turned the Formless Ones to black goo?"

Sighing, I said, "Yeah, but when he asked me to recreate it, I couldn't. Not even a spark of light."

James frowned. "Hmmm. Well, it will come,

maybe it has something specifically to do with the threat of the Formless Ones."

I shrugged. "Maybe?" Shaking my head I said, "I just don't know. It feels different when I'm training than when I use it against them. I can't really explain it in words."

"Maybe you just need more practice. We could get the group together again and practice like we did last year," James suggested. "You know they aren't going to teach us to use more powerful stuff, they don't want us starting anything and taking over." He chuckled.

I smiled and snuggled into his arms. "True. But I think we'll hold off on getting everyone together, we don't really have a place to practice, since I can't exactly leave the school building."

"Yeah, that's true." James sighed. "Are you coming over to the vampire dorms after your session with Professor Ubel?"

"Yes." I smiled. "I've got plans with Jodie, we're going to play pool and then watch the next episode of *Stranger Things*. We're trying to pace ourselves so we don't have to wait so long for then next season," I said with a laugh. "Do you want to do something after?"

"Are you staying over at our dorms for the weekend?" he asked.

"Maybe. I don't like being alone in my room, even if it is warded to the hilt. It's just lonely. And I do feel safer here. Hela can't help but make anyone feel safe under her watch." I grinned.

"Hela is good at making everyone feel safe," James agreed. "How about I pick us, well *you*, up dinner in town and bring it back here. Since I can't take you out, we'll have a picnic in my room before lights out and then you can stay with Jodie for the rest of the night."

I stopped and turned to face him, a smile on my lips as I pushed up on my toes and kissed his soft lips. "You are seriously the best boyfriend a girl could ask for." I grinned as he gripped my waist and pulled me back in for another breathless kiss.

"And don't you forget it," he said with a chuckle.

Professor Ubel gently held a box in his hands in front of me. "Now, my dear girl, when I set this box down, and open the lid, take a deep breath and do exactly what I said. Draw in the energy from the being, and around the room. Form it in your mind into a solid shield of light, and then project it at the being."

I nodded and tried to concentrate. This was the

fourth time we'd tried this particular spell and I had so far been able to create nothing but a brief gust of wind before my focus lapsed and the creature pounced on me before dissipating. It was after all merely energy in the form of whatever creature Professor Ubel thought might encourage me to get the spell right.

"Alright, I'm ready," I said, giving him a nod.

Professor Ubel set the box down, and then flipped the lid back. This time, a Black Annis crawled from the box. My heartbeat began to speed up and I began pulling energy from the creature and then from the room. In my head, I pictured the wall of bright shimmering white light. I held it for a moment and then released the image of the light with my hands at the Black Annis.

This time the spell built up, starting to shimmer and then fell into more of a misty fog. The Black Annis pushed through it and came straight at me. The moment it made contact it evaporated and I dropped to the ground on my knees panting.

"Not too bad. Take a moment and we'll try again," he commented as he picked up the box and moved to the table to set it all up again.

I sighed, feeling drained, but nodded and did the best I could to draw back my focus, ready to go again.

ONCE I FINISHED WITH PROFESSOR UBEL, I WAS more frustrated than I had been before I started working with him. The spell he was teaching me wasn't working and the most I'd managed to do was create a shimmering smoke screen that did nothing to stop or block the creature from getting to me, let alone kill it. Hardly useful. Professor Ubel had said I was making progress, but it sure didn't feel that way.

With a sigh, I trudged down the hall to my dorm room. I checked the wards to make sure they were still active and then I entered and tossed my books on my desk. As I grabbed a change of clothes from the closet, I took a moment to stare at the empty side of it. I hadn't bothered to move any of my stuff into the spot, hoping that Helen would come back. But Helen, like Helen's stuff was gone. She wasn't coming back. She hardly spoke to me anymore, even in class. I sat down on my bed blinking back tears.

There was a knock at the door and I looked up. *Who would be bothering with me?* I thought, feeling depressed.

"Who is it?"

"Porta. Can I come in?"

I rose from the bed and opened the door. "Sure. What's up?"

Porta stepped in the room and looked around, fidgeting as if the room made her uncomfortable. "Uh." She looked at me as I went back to sit on my bed. "Well, we wondered if you'd wanna come to the movies with us. Luci, Helen and me, I mean."

I gave her a half smile. "Luci sent you, didn't she?" I asked, knowing I was right.

"Well, yeah. She said she could feel that you were lonely." Porta frowned. "We haven't been very good friends since the basketball incident. I'm sorry."

"It's okay. I haven't exactly made it easy with all the weirdness that keeps happening around me."

"Yeah, but that's not your fault." Porta smiled. "So what do you say? Movies?"

"As much as I would love to, I can't. I'm still not allowed to leave the school building. Let alone go out into public."

"Well that sucks eggs." Porta frowned. "Well we could do something here... get the guys and maybe have a video game competition? Or maybe go to the gym and play basketball there?"

"Thanks, but not tonight. You three go, have a good time. You don't have to entertain me." I smiled. "Actually, I'm supposed to hang out with Jodie tonight, so I wouldn't be able to go with you even if I wasn't under house arrest."

"Oh." Porta frowned as if she hadn't thought I'd

made plans with anyone other than James. As if it came as a surprise that I was still friends with the other vampires now that I wasn't living over there. And then she smiled. "Well good, I'm glad you are still friends with her. I guess I knew that you were, it's just y'all are so different... I mean with you being a — nevermind. I'm rambling." She laughed. "How about tomorrow then? We could, I don't know—"

Porta got an odd look on her face, as if she was having a conversation in her head.

"I'll ask her, Luci, just give me a minute, geez." Porta shook her head. "Luci suggested a slumber party for tomorrow since you can't go with us tonight. What do you say?"

I grinned. "I'd like that."

"Great, we'll pop some popcorn, pull up some campy scary movies on Hulu or Netflix and have a good time. It is Halloween time after all. We should do something together on Halloween, don't you think?"

"Totally. Witches should be together on Halloween." I grinned. "Maybe we can have a party in the witches' common room, invite the vampires, and just have a good time. Think the professors will let us?"

"Probably. It sounds like the start of a great plan. We'll get it all sorted tomorrow night," Porta replied, a twinkle in her eye. "I'd better go, Luci and Helen are waiting for me. Come over to our room around four tomorrow, okay?"

"Okay," I agreed and then stopped thinking of Helen. "Um, you're sure Helen is going to be okay with me being there overnight?"

Porta smiled. "Yeah, she'll be fine. I think she'd come back here, if, you know, things stay as calm as they have been."

That had me grinning. "Then I will do my best to keep it calm."

Porta laughed. "Okay, girl, I'll see ya tomorrow." She opened the door and headed out.

I had a grin on my face as Porta closed the door behind her. Suddenly I wasn't feeling depressed at all and I was looking forward to both this weekend's activities and the ones we hoped to plan for Halloween. I quickly changed clothes and packed a small backpack before heading over to the vampire dorms. I was feeling much better now than I had been when I first got to my room. Just because I was feeling lonely, didn't mean I had to be alone. I had friends, both witches and vampires.

I passed by Lukas in the hallway and gave the Russian vampire a small wave. "Hey, Lukas!" I called as I continued on to the vampire's common room.

"Staying the weekend, little witch?" he asked

gruffly, but he had a smile on his lips and a twinkle in his eyes.

"Yes, tonight and probably some of tomorrow, but not the whole weekend."

He nodded. "Have fun, little witch."

I smiled as I cut through the commons and into the hallway that led to Jodie's room.

"Elsku dúllan mín, what brings you to visit us this day?" Hela greeted me in the hallway, a large grin on her Icelandic face. Hela was the vampire girls' dorm monitor and had a special way of handling all those in her charge.

"Good evening, Hela," I said looking up at her six-foot four frame with a smile. "I'm here to spend some time with Jodie. We're going to hang out for a while, and then I'm having a picnic with James. I'll be staying with Jodie later tonight though too, is that alright?"

"Já auðvitað, we are always glad to have you with us, sweet one," Hela said giving me a hug.

"Thanks, Hela," I replied. "Is Jodie in her room?" I asked looking down the hallway.

"Já, she is," Hela said, "I'll leave you to it, sweet one. I have my rounds to make. If you need me, just knock, I'll be here. Nobody would dare send anything in here to get you with me keeping watch over you."

Hela stroked my hair and kissed the top of my head in a motherly way.

"Thank you, Hela." I smiled up at her and then continued down the hall to Jodie's room.

I knocked on the door and waited. Jodie opened it a moment later, a smile on her face. She wore a pair of purple and white striped leggings and a long purple sweater that came to mid-thigh. She wore no socks or footwear over her hooves. Her horns were dyed purple to match her outfit and her long black hair hung in waves down her back. I noticed she'd dyed the ends of her hair a bright purple as well.

"Love the hair, I've been tempted to do something like that," I said with a grin.

Jodie arched a brow and grinned. "I'm in, you just say the word and I will fix you right up."

I laughed. "Not tonight."

"Okay, but when you're ready, you'll ask me, right?"

I grinned. "I wouldn't dare ask anyone else."

"Great! Ready to play some pool?" she asked.

I nodded and handed her my backpack. "I am, though I'm not very good. Felt I should warn you." I laughed as she tossed my pack on the spare bed in her room that had been mine last year.

Jodie laughed too. "No worries, I'll help you if you need it. You know, you didn't have to bring a bag, you could have borrowed something of mine, again." She grinned as she pulled the door closed behind us.

"I know, but I feel bad when I don't get it back to you in a timely manner." I laughed.

"Like I even notice," Jodie deadpanned. "I have like a million outfits, and it was just that once that you forgot." Her laugh tinkled through the hallway.

"Yeah but you had to come looking for it, because I forgot all about it." I hung my head and recalled her turning up in the middle of the night looking for her favorite green sweater that I'd borrowed.

"Well, it was the one Terrance bought me, so I wanted to wear it for our date that night." She grinned.

"Terr bought it? Oh my god, how did I not know that? I never would have borrowed it if you'd said!" I blushed and then my eyes grew wide. "That's why he complimented it that day! And I just thanked him and said it was yours!"

Jodie chuckled. "I know. He about had a fit that I'd lent it to you." She grinned. "I more than made up for it though." She winked, a naughty look on her face.

"I don't even want to know," I said with a laugh.

We entered the commons and headed to the pool table. Some of the male vampires watched us as we set up the table, their eyes on Jodie's behind as she lined up her first shot. "Eyes off the merchandise, fellas, this booty is taken," she commented as she broke the balls, scattering them around the table. She whirled around and arched a brow at them, a smirk on her lips.

"Just admiring your form, Jodie," one of the vampires, a Strigoi I thought, said. He wore a smirk and ran his hand through his dark hair. "Can't help but admire pretty girls like the two of you, right guys?"

I blushed as I attempted to hit the white ball, but totally scratched when it went in the pocket instead of hitting the red ball I'd been aiming at.

"Pretty sure James would be happy to rearrange your face for checking out his girl, like you are Matthew, you might want to dial back the flirting." Jodie grinned. "Now, let us play, and you get back to your game. When it's over, Bethany and I call dibs on the TV we have *Stranger Things* to watch."

"I'm a strange thing, you two can watch me anytime you want, sweet thangs," Matthew commented.

I laughed at the cheesy comment and his eyes lit up.

"It's your funeral, dude," Jodie replied, her eyes going to the door where James stood, his eyes narrowed on Matthew.

"You wanna repeat that?" James asked, arching his brow.

I swallowed my grin and turned back to the table.

"Just kidding around, James, no need to get in a huff," Matthew uttered, turning back to the game.

I felt James come up behind me as I bent over to line up my next shot. He gripped my hips and leaned over me, whispering in my ear, "Pull back gently," he kissed my neck, "steady your shot," his lips brushed my earlobe, "push forward."

I did as he said, tamping down the surge of pleasure coursing through me at his gentle touch and brush of lips. The white ball rolled across the table and hit the red ball, knocking it into the pocket in the corner. Raising up, I turned in his arms and kissed him. "Thank you."

"My pleasure," he murmured, his hands still on my waist.

"Okay, break it up, you two. This is supposed to be my time with her, James." Jodie frowned at him.

"I know. I just came in to say hello before I head into town. I'm picking up dinner for Bethany." He smiled.

"Well, you've said your hello. Now go. That game is almost over and we've got things to do."

James chuckled. "I know. I'll be back later with your Kung Po Chicken and lo mein." He lifted me up by my ass a little and then kissed my lips gently. "See you later."

I blushed and nodded as he moved away. I followed him with my eyes until he was out of the room.

"Girl, you've got it so bad." Jodie laughed and bumped my hip with hers.

Laughing, I bumped her right back. "You're one to talk! Don't think I haven't seen you with Terrance," I commented.

"True." She took her shot, sinking the yellow stripe ball. "He is pretty darn sexy, especially when he kisses me."

"Ew, T-M-I, Jodie," I joked.

Jodie laughed and all the guys in front of the TV looked over at us, their eyes focused on her. She shook her head and rolled her eyes. "Ignore them. I do."

We finished our game and started another while we waited for the TV. Thirty minutes later the guys all stood and stretched, taking their time evacuating from the room. The lingered, as if hoping one of us would suggest they stay to keep us company, but eventually they left. Once they were gone, we put away the pool cues and balls and then headed over to the couches. Jodie pulled up *Netflix* and found our show.

"What episode are we on? I can't remember."

"Season one, episode four," I replied settling into the couch. "They just found a body, remember? They think it's Will."

"Oh yeah." Jodie nodded. She found the right episode and we settled back to watch.

I left Bethany playing pool with Jodie, trusting her to keep her safe from the likes of Matthew. He was mostly harmless, I knew, but he was still a vampire. I had no worries about Bethany leaving me for another vampire, she was mine and they all knew it. Which also meant I could trust them to keep their teeth off of her too. With a grin, I headed off campus to meet up with Cory at the comic book store.

The bell jingled as I stepped into the shop. There were bins filled with comic books and racks lining the walls with all the newest editions. The bins held back copies. Multiples of old favorites and sorted by the universe and the series. Cory was in front of the *DC Universe* section. He looked up when I came in.

"Hey, didn't think you were coming." Cory went back to flipping through the bin.

"I'm not staying long. Just wasting time until I have to go order dinner for Bethany."

Cory shook his head and grinned. "Man, you are so whipped." He chuckled.

I rolled my eyes at him. "Laugh it up, breeze boy. One day you'll find your match and then I'll have a field day teasing the shit out of you."

Cory's black eyes glittered like onyx as he glanced up at me and then flipped me off. "Never gonna happen. No chick is gonna take my heart."

"Yeah, sure." I replied, a grin on my lips. "I'm gonna check for the new *Border Town* release." I headed over to the *Vertigo* section on the wall and found what I was looking for. The series was about a town on the border between two worlds where monsters from Mexican folklore invaded the town. It was pretty cool, and I liked the concept of it. The artwork was pretty good too.

After finding the most current copy of *Border Town*, I browsed and picked up the latest copies of *Venom*, *Thor*, and another by *Vertigo* called *The Dreaming*. I turned to Cory and holding up the stack, I said, "Hey man, I got mine, I'm gonna head out, pick up the food and go back to campus to meet up with Bethany. We're having a picnic in our room, so..." I let my words drift off with a grin.

"Yeah, yeah, just text me when I'm allowed back in the room. Geez I hate the weekends when you have Bethany over. You're always kicking me out, man." Cory frowned at me.

I grinned. "Telling you, dude, as soon as you get a girl—"

"Yeah, yeah, just go already!" Cory muttered and rolled his eyes.

Chuckling, I headed to the counter. After paying and picking up my brown paper bag filled with comics, I headed down the street to the *China Star.* I pulled open the doors and smiled at the guy behind the counter.

"Ummm, what can I do for you, sir?" He looked at me curiously.

I smiled and said, "Yeah, can I get an order of Kung Po Chicken, with lo mein, the sweet and sour soup, and a couple of egg rolls?"

The guy stared at me, shock all over his face. "But you're a—" he stopped speaking and looked around probably not wanting to be overheard by his customers.

I arched a brow, wondering how he knew what I was. "I am, yes, and?" I replied frowning. "It's for my girlfriend," I continued, hoping he wasn't finding me some kind of threat.

He blinked at me for a moment and then I felt it, he had magic. He was a witch, which had to be how he knew what I was. "Right. Sorry. We just don't get many of you in here." The guy nodded.

I shrugged. "We don't generally have a need to come in. I'm doing something nice for my girl."

"I'll get that for you, be right back with your order."

"Thanks." I sat on the bench by the register to wait.

"Hey, James!"

I looked up and noticed a table of witches in the near empty restaurant. "Hey, Terrance. What's up?" I asked, going over to them.

"Not much, where's Bethany?"

"Hanging out with Jodie, why?"

"Oh, yeah, forgot they were doing that," Terrance said with a chuckle. "Want to join us?" He nodded at the empty chair at their table.

I looked at the other two guys, Finch and Quinn. "Hey guys," I acknowledged them with a smile. "Thanks, but I'm just picking up dinner for Bethany and then we're going to spend the evening together after she and Jodie are done with their show."

"Yeah I'm meeting up with Jodie at nine," Terrance commented.

"Sir?" the guy from the counter was back with a bag.

"Looks like I've got to go." I gave them a wave. "Catch ya'll later."

I went to the counter and paid. "Thank you," I gave him a smile.

"Anytime. Here, take a menu, it's got our phone number on it, next time, if you call, we can have it ready for you." He handed me the menu.

"Great, thanks." I put it in the bag and grabbed a set of utensils as well as chopsticks from the side table next to the counter for take-out customers, not knowing which Bethany would prefer. Once I had everything, I gave the guys a wave and then made my way back to the school.

As I walked, I looked around for any of the automaton that attacked whenever Bethany went out, but I didn't see anything. Nor did I hear any of the tell-tale ticking sounds that accompanied their presence. I half wished we could take our picnic up to the clock tower, as it was our favorite spot on campus, but it was too risky. And I would not risk Bethany for anything.

With the food in hand, I entered the building and made my way to the common room to see if Bethany was finished with her show. When I entered, she looked up and smiled. The look on her face when she saw me always made my heart melt. I knew I was falling for this girl hard. I lifted up the bag and grinned.

"Are you ready for dinner?" I asked.

She hopped up off the couch and skipped over to me. "I am. We were just discussing the show. See you later, Jodie?" She looked over at her friend.

"I'm headed out with Terrance at nine, so I won't be in till late. I'll try not to wake you when I come in." She chuckled.

"Okay, bye," Bethany replied with a grin.

We walked together back to my room where I pulled a blanket down off the shelf of the closet and set it out on the floor. We both sat down and I began to lay out her food and hand her the utensils and chopsticks. "I wasn't sure which you'd want."

"I like the chopsticks, but I'm glad you got the others too. It's kind of hard to eat soup with them." She laughed.

I felt the sound of it in my soul. I looked over at her and grinned. "Eat, I'll put on some music."

She nodded and started in on the cartons of chicken and lo mein, expertly using the chopsticks as she ate. "Mmmm, this is good."

"I saw some of your friends there, Terrance, Finch and Quinn."

"Yeah, Jodie said they were going out for a while so we could have some girl time."

I flipped through one of the comics I'd picked up, but I wasn't really reading it. It was just something to do while she ate.

"What's that?" she asked, wiping her mouth on a napkin and then picking up an eggroll.

I turned the cover toward her. "Thor?"

"Ah, the hot god of thunder with the hammer, right?" she teased.

"*Hot*?" I arched a brow at her.

She laughed and took a bite of her eggroll. Once she finished chewing, she leaned over and kissed me. "Just kidding. You are hot, and mine," she whispered before kissing me again.

"I am," I agreed, pulling her to me, kissing her harder.

When we pulled apart we were both breathless and panting.

"Finish your dinner," I breathed out, pressing my forehead to hers. "Or I might decide to finish this..."

She pulled back a heartbeat later, her cheeks a beautiful rosy color.

"I love looking at you like this," I murmured, my finger stroking her cheek. "So beautiful."

Bethany looked down, her cheeks still pink as her lashes fluttered down, hiding her eyes from me. She smiled and then peeked up at me, biting her lip. My eyes were drawn to her action and I could feel my heartrate pick up as I focused on her reddening lips.

I blinked, disturbing the image in my mind. Shaking my head I smiled and turned away. I moved over to my desk and picked up the next book in the Harry Potter series. "I thought we could read some more."

"I'd like that," Bethany agreed.

When she finished, I cleaned everything up, and then we snuggled together on my bed. I opened the book and began to read.

The next week was a whirlwind of planning with Helen, Porta and Luci. We got permission from Professor Zin to have a Halloween party and invite the vampires. She and Professor Corbett were going to chaperone, but they had us move the party to the cafeteria. That way there would be plenty of room and the nursing station wasn't too far off if any of the vampires needed to go get a quick bite to eat.

Helen, Porta and Luci had gone into town to pick out party supplies and I'd been sad that I couldn't join them, but James had cheered me up by bringing me ice cream that afternoon, so it worked out. We'd planned the party for Halloween night, which luckily fell on a Saturday. It gave us all day to decorate the cafeteria.

"Did you find a DJ?" Porta asked as I helped her put up the orange and black streamers.

"Yeah, James helped. He said one of the vampires was pretty good, and they have the equipment. He'll be in at four to start setting up. James is going to help him get set up."

"Great. I was wondering how we were going to get one out here, being that we are a school filled with scary creatures," Porta said with a laugh.

"The only thing scary here are those stupid creepy spiders and bats, but mostly the spiders!" Helen shuddered.

I'm glad there haven't been any more incidents with them, Luci said in our heads.

"Yeah, but only because Bethany hasn't gone outside in over a month!" Helen replied. "Sorry Bethany."

"It's okay. And you're not wrong. If I even step a foot out the doors they are on me like gangbusters. I don't know why." I frowned. "It sucks being stuck inside though."

Porta rubbed my shoulder and smiled. "The professors and Dusk Knights will figure it out."

I nodded. "Hopefully."

"Enough talk about that, we've got a ton of stuff to do still! I'm going to head into the kitchen and check on the snacks for the party." Helen got off her ladder and headed off in the direction of the kitchen.

❦

"HAVING A GOOD TIME?" JAMES WHISPERED IN MY ear as we danced hours later.

The cafeteria had been transformed into Halloween Party Central. There was a reflective disco ball with colored lights in the center of the room, spinning and flashing everywhere. Jack-o-lanterns with candles adorned every table along with alternating black and orange table cloths. The tables closest to the kitchen held giant bowls of chips, platters of cookies shaped like Halloween monsters and orange sherbet punch and glasses. The center of the room had been cleared for dancing and Matthew, as it turned out was the DJ that James had spoken of, was dressed as Frankenstein and manning a table on the edge of the room blaring out a mix of music.

More than half of the students had dressed up for the occasion. I was dressed as Little Red Riding Hood, and James was dressed as a wolf with his own fangs out and showing. He made for a cute wolf and he didn't scare me in the least.

"I am," I replied. "I'm so glad we were able to do this and it all came together so quickly."

James grinned. "Witches and vampires working together can create great things." He laughed.

"True," I agreed with a grin.

The song ended and he grabbed my hand. "Need some punch, Red?"

I nodded and we headed over to the table with the refreshments. James filled a cup and handed it to me. "Thank you."

He leaned in and kissed my cheek.

Professor Zin walked by, dressed as a scarecrow, but at three and a half feet tall, she wasn't very scary for a scarecrow. At least not until she barked, "None of that now, Miss Welch, Mr. Barret!"

"Yes, ma'am!" we replied and chuckled.

I tossed my empty cup in the trash and we headed back to the dance floor. The rest of the evening went by much too quickly. Most of the professors put in an appearance, though none of them were dressed up for the occasion. I was thankful that Professor Chalcedony kept his distance. He'd spent the week complaining about the dance where witches and vampire scum were going to be mingling and having a good time. He'd called it an abomination. None of us paid him any attention.

We'd all taken to ignoring his rants in class and not letting him get to any of us. I was especially impressed by James and the rest of the Strigoi who didn't rise to his baiting. Instead they held their heads high and did everything requested of them, even when the homework was meant to degrade them. It seemed to enrage the professor even more that not one of them reacted to his bigotry.

"Last song, party witches and vamps!" Matthew called out. "Well go with the best Halloween song on the planet... Everybody do the *Monster Mash*!"

With a laugh, we all danced, our hands in the air like giant paws and did as he suggested. When the song ended, everyone clapped and helped clean up the cafeteria. I noticed that Consuela, who was dressed as the Bride of Frankenstein, was helping Matthew pack up his equipment and chatting animatedly with him. It made me smile.

"Think it's another match?" I whispered to James, directing his attention toward the DJ table.

He narrowed his gaze and said, "Man, I hope so. He needs to stop hitting on every girl he sees. Maybe Consuela is strong enough to keep him in line." He grinned.

I rolled my eyes. "You're not wrong, he is a flirt, but he's harmless... for a vampire." I laughed. "I think once he realizes he's got her attention, the excessive flirting will die down."

"It better," James growled playfully.

I laughed again and kissed his wolf shaped nose. "Come on you, we've got more to clean-up."

"Ugh, how did we end up on this cleanup crew?"

I arched a brow at him and grinned. "Because your girlfriend was in on the planning committee and assured the professors that we would be sure to have the cafeteria back to normal before tomorrow."

"Huh. Yeah, I guess that is a good reason." He pulled me close to him, streamers of orange and black still in my hands. "Does that mean I can't steal a kiss until this is all cleaned?"

I grinned. "You can steal as many kisses as you'd like, so long as Professor Zin doesn't see."

James looked around sneakily, and then leaned in and kissed me, leaving me breathless once again. I was walking on air for the rest of the time it took to clean up the room.

After another hour of clean up, I was wiped out and collapsed into James' arms with a sigh.

"Your dorm or are you staying with Jodie?" James asked.

"Mine I think." I glanced up at him slyly. "You want to stay?"

James arched a brow and smirked. "You think the professors won't be paying attention?"

I shrugged. "They tend to leave me alone. All except Professor Singh, and she seemed pretty occupied with those Dusk Knights tonight. I heard her talking to one of them earlier when you made a run to the nursing station. Something is going on out on the west side of campus."

James got a serious look on his face. "Should I go check it out, you think?"

"No, let them handle it. We're students, they should be handling all this anyway."

"I know, but I worry about it being a threat to you."

I smiled up at him. "I know. But if you're with me, I'll be fine."

"Sneaky. Now I have to stay with you." He pulled me close.

I laughed. "Well... you were going to anyway," I murmured.

"True." He chuckled.

CHAPTER 26

BETHANY

After Halloween, everything went back to normal once again. Another month passed, and we planned a Thanksgiving feast in the cafeteria. Since the vampires didn't eat, they bowed out of the occasion.

I ate a huge plate of turkey, stuffing, potatoes and green beans. And for dessert we had several different kinds of pies. I hate to admit it, but I ate three slices, one pumpkin, one apple and one pecan. They were so good. After dinner I went back to my room and called Dad.

"Hi, sweetheart, Happy Thanksgiving," Dad said when he answered the phone.

"Hi, Daddy. Happy Thanksgiving to you," I said with a smile. "Are you and Mom still eating?"

Dad sighed. "No, your mom went to Aunt Susan's

for Thanksgiving, so I stayed home and watched the game."

"What? You didn't have a feast?" I felt bad that he'd missed out.

"Well, I did cook a turkey, and I picked up a pie at Wal-Mart, so I don't think I missed out. I didn't want to go to Aunt Susan's and listen to Uncle Jim tell me that we were crazy to send you to that expensive private boarding school again. You know how he is. Besides, your mom and Aunt Susan were planning to go to all the Black Friday sales that started at nine, and then I'd have been left with Uncle Jim. No thanks." He chuckled.

I grinned. "Well, did you at least enjoy your turkey and pie?"

"I did. It's been a pretty good, quiet day. Oh, before I forget, I had a talk with your mother and she has decided to allow you to continue to see James. Not that you were going to stop anyway, but at least now she won't nag you as much about it."

"Seriously?" I asked brightly, feeling a bit relieved that I wouldn't have to argue with her anymore.

"Seriously." I could hear the grin in his voice. "Did you have a good day?"

"I did. We had a big feast, and I ate three kinds of pie. I'm stuffed and exhausted." I laughed.

"Well good. I'm glad you are having a good year,

sweetheart. I'll let you go now, get some rest and we'll see you soon, okay?"

"Okay, Daddy. Love you."

"Love you too, sweetheart."

I hung up the phone and got ready for bed. It had been a fun night, and I was exhausted but I really missed spending the evening with James. With a sigh, I climbed into bed.

WE'D HAD NO MORE SIGHTINGS OF THE SPIDERS OR bats around campus, and nothing strange had gone on since my last encounter with my possessed phone and the battle in the courtyard when the chupacabra had protected me. I still hesitated going outside because Professor Singh and her Dusk Knights still hadn't figured out who was behind the automatons. Instead I found things to do indoors.

Classes had ended for the week, being a Friday, so I was headed down to the vampire commons to hang out with Jodie, Lily and Noor. Fira was going to join us later for a movie marathon. We were watching the *Twilight Saga*. They all thought it was absolutely hysterical that the vampires in it sparkled. Aside from the sparkling, I felt a connection to *Bella*, seeing as I was, well, mostly mortal like her and dating a vampire. But first, we were playing darts.

"So where is James this evening?" Noor asked as she picked up her first dart.

"He and Cory went into town."

"And you didn't go with?" Lily asked curiously.

I shook my head. "No, I'm under house arrest, remember?" I commented smirking.

"You're not." Lily laughed.

"Feels like it." I shrugged. "Anyway, I told him to go, no need for both of us to be stir-crazy."

"Yeah," Jodie agreed. "I think I would hate to be in your shoes. Not being able to leave the building? That has to suck."

"You're not kidding. Stupid automatons."

"Maybe their gone? We haven't seen any evidence of them in months now," Jodie suggested.

"I'm not taking any chances. Professor Singh still doesn't know who created them, or who possessed my phone. So until she does, I'm staying here. Where it's safe."

"Yeah, with a bunch of vampires," Jodie teased. "Safe."

I giggled.

"What do they want with you anyway?" Noor asked.

I shrugged. "I don't know. It's not like I can ask

them, it's the Shadow Society, not as if I can ask them for an invitation to come and speak to them," I commented with a laugh.

"The Shadow Society?" Noor's already large eyes grew wide. "They are the ones behind all this?"

I shrugged. "I don't know for sure, but it feels like it. I can't think of anyone else who would want to kill me just because I have more power than them. Who else could it be?"

"True, can't possibly be anyone else..."

"Unless you know of a witch serial killer out there who is really bad at their job?" I said deadpan and then grinned.

They all laughed.

"Well at least you haven't lost your sense of humor," Lily replied. "Now, who's going first?"

"How about we each throw a dart, closest to the bulls-eye goes first."

"Sounds good."

We each stood shoulder to shoulder and aimed, throwing all at once.

"Hah! I go first!" Jodie called.

"I'm second closest, Noor what happened?" Lily asked, looking at the wall where a green feathered dart protruded.

"I was distracted," she commented, her gaze

straying to Tran and Kale who were watching football on the big screen.

I laughed and she faded a bit, and then shimmered back into existence. "They are a handsome distraction, I agree." I smiled at her.

Our game went on until the boys finished their game and Fira came in and demanded the TV. "Okay, you're finished! We have sparkling vampires to watch, so get out!"

"Ugh, can't believe you are going to defile our TV with that stuff!" Kale commented, but we all knew he was just teasing his sister.

"You will not knock the glory that is *Edward Cullen*!" Fira fired back, her hands on her hips.

Chuckling, Tran and Kale left.

"Ah, now that they've gone, who is ready for the *Twilight* marathon?" Fira asked, putting in the first DVD.

"Me!" Noor replied, tossing her last dart over her shoulder and hitting the bulls-eye.

"How did you do that?" Lily stared at her. "Why couldn't you have done that in the game?"

Noor shrugged and flopped down on the couch. "Luck?"

Shaking her head, Lily sighed. She kicked off her shoes and settled down next to her.

"Do you need anything?" Jodie asked, looking at me. "Popcorn?"

"Oh, popcorn, yeah, that sounds good."

Nodding, she said, "Don't start yet, we're grabbing popcorn for Bethany!"

We went over to a bar like area that was set up with a sink, a microwave and cabinets filled with mugs, bowls and snacks. The vampires started keeping nonperishable snacks here for me last year. And now they continued with it for Terrance, Consuela and the few other witches who came over to visit the vampires too. She pulled out a bag of Orville Redenbacher and opened it. She set it in the microwave and less than five minutes later we had popcorn.

"Come on." Jodie grabbed my hand and we practically flew back to the couch and slammed down on it without spilling any of the buttery popcorn.

The marathon was fun and didn't end till well after three A.M. I ended up crashing in Jodie's room and didn't wake up until about three the next afternoon. Borrowing a pair of jeans from Fira, since Jodie's would never fit me, and a top from Jodie, I jumped in the girls' shower and then dressed. I was starving, so I slipped back into the commons area and pulled some snack cakes from the cabinet.

"Hello, beautiful," James said, slipping his hands

around my waist as he kissed my neck. "Did you have a good time?"

Taking a bite of the cake, I nodded. I swallowed and said, "I did. Did you?"

James shrugged. "Yeah, we didn't do much, just went to the movies and then to the comic store."

"It was open that late?" I asked.

"It was only nine. They stay open till ten. We got back here around eleven, you all were busy drooling over the Cullen clan, so we left you to it and went back to our room with our new comic stash." He chuckled, teasing me.

I blushed and ducked my head to his chest.

"You're so pretty when you turn pink like that," he teased.

"Stop," I said laughing.

He kissed my head and I looked up at him, smiling. He took advantage of that and kissed me properly, pulling me close and squishing the rest of my cake between us.

I pulled back and sighed. "Jodie is not gonna be happy with you."

James chuckled. "Why?"

"Because this is her shirt."

"Oh." He laughed. "It will come out, no need to worry. Come on, I'll give you one of mine." He took my hand and led me to his room. "Hey, Cory, could you leave for a minute?"

"What?" He looked at us. "Why?"

"Bethany needs to change her shirt, she's a very messy eater."

"I am not!" I exclaimed. "James squished my cake into me!"

James just shook his head and sighed. "It's okay, beautiful, I like that you're a messy eater."

I growled at him and he laughed.

"Yeah, I think I believe Bethany, 'specially since she's not the only one with cake all over her shirt." Cory chuckled. "I'll give ya five, man, but no more, so no getting all handsy up in here. This is where I have to sleep. Don't want that image in my head!"

James shucked his shirt and threw it at him, but Cory caught it and dropped it in the hamper next to the door. Before he shut it, he flipped us off and laughed.

James shook his head, laughing. He opened his dresser, pulled out a *Braves* baseball tee with three quarter sleeves, and handed it to me. "Here. It might be a little long, but it will do."

"Thank you." I smiled and turned my back, slipping out of Jodie's shirt and into the tee. I turned back around and held my arms out. The sleeves reached almost to my wrists and the tail of the shirt went almost to mid-thigh, but other than that, it fit all right.

"Mmmm, the *Braves* never looked so good," James murmured.

I blushed again, but didn't turn away. I was too captivated by his naked chest.

He seemed to notice and arched a brow at me, grinning. "See something you like, beautiful?" He rubbed his hand over his broad chest. "Sorry, no sparkles..." He held his arms out wide.

I laughed and moved into his embrace. "I think I prefer you without sparkles, just so you know."

"Good, because I have to tell you, glitter is a pain in the ass to get off and I don't really want to have to go through that again."

I looked up at him and laughed. "Again?"

He grinned. "A story for another day?"

"Oh, no, I think I want to hear that story now," I replied.

With a fake sigh, he proceeded to say, "It was after the last movie came out. Cory thought it would be funny if we went as the Cullens for Halloween."

I tried really hard not to laugh, but I wasn't successful. I burst out laughing so loud that Cory came back in the room to see what was going on. He took one look at James and then grinned.

"Dude, when a girl laughs at you because you've taken your shirt off, it's time to hit the gym."

James picked up a pillow and slammed it into Cory's face. "Yeah, I was telling her about the year we went as the Cullens for Halloween!"

"Oh crap! That glitter took forever to get out! I think I was still wiping it off at New Years!"

I laughed so hard I had tears running down my cheeks and I couldn't breathe. I fanned my face, trying to calm down. "Oh that is too funny!"

"I'm glad you think so!" Cory chuckled. "I don't think Lindon forgave us for like a year for the mess we made. That glitter went everywhere."

James pulled another shirt from his dresser, a solid black v-neck tee, and put it on. He flopped down on his bed and pulled me down with him. "So, beautiful, what are your plans for tonight?"

"I don't know, kinda planned to stick around here, Jodie's going out with Terrance, but she said I could crash in her room again."

"Good, maybe we should go get you food first though?" He looked at me. "Seeing as I smushed your cake."

"Yes please." I smiled.

He nodded and slid off the bed, then held his hand out for me. "Cors, we'll see you later."

Cory held up his comic and said, "I'll be here."

SOPHIE CASTLE

We headed up to the dining hall where I ate a bowl of chicken and dumplings, and then we returned to the vampire common room where we spent the rest of the evening just enjoying each other's company and watching *The Haunting of Hill House* on *Netflix*.

MONDAY MORNING I WAS DRAGGING, STILL TIRED after spending the weekend basically on vampire time. I could barely keep my eyes open for Professor Singh's class and almost got caught falling asleep instead of practicing my wards.

"Bethany," Helen hissed, jostling my arm.

"What?" I blinked at her.

"You were practically snoring," she murmured. "Professor Singh won't be happy if she catches you napping."

I nodded. "Yeah, sorry. Thanks for catching me."

"Why are you so tired?" Helen asked. "Are you not sleeping because of—" she looked around the room and lowered her voice even more, "the spiders?"

"Oh, I haven't had a problem with them since Professor Singh took care of the door and window. No, I just spent the entire weekend in the vampire dorms and my sleep is all messed up."

"Oh." Helen nodded, a slight frown marring her face. "Well, good."

I smiled. "You could come back you know," I put out there, hoping she would.

"Yeah, maybe," she said as the bell rang ending class. "I-I gotta go. I'll see you later."

Sighing, I nodded and gathered my books. I made my way sluggishly to Professor Chalcedony's class. It might be the one class I shared with James, but it was definitely my least favorite and that was all due to the Professor. If it were say Professor Zin or Professor Corbett even teaching it, I think I would have enjoyed it. I walked into the room right as the bell rang.

"Cutting it close, Miss Welch! Perhaps I should give you detention!"

"Sorry, Professor," I said taking my seat, blinking back tears. He wasn't a nice man and always berated us, but mostly his abuse focused on the Strigoi and me. The witches in the class mostly flew under the radar.

To prove that point, Lars Mueller rushed in the door a second later and smiled at the professor. "Sorry, Professor, I was speaking with Professor Zin."

"Very well, Mr. Mueller, take your seat."

I just shook my head and sighed.

"Problem, Miss Welch?" He narrowed his eyes on me.

"No, Professor." I slid down in my seat, slouching, trying to make myself a smaller target.

It didn't seem to help. Professor Chalcedony seemed to just get angrier and angrier, screaming at me about what a poor excuse of a witch I was. I was near tears when James spoke up.

"Professor, I think that is really uncalled for! She is a student, and you are a teacher!"

I glanced up and a wave of fear hit me as I looked in the professor's eyes. They seemed crazed and when he turned his insane gaze on James, whispering, I knew something was wrong.

All of a sudden, things around the room began to animate and I just stared in shock.

Professor Chalcedony was attacking us!

CHAPTER 27

BETHANY

I stared in horror as James' desk came alive and he jumped from it. And then the rest of the Strigois' desks did the same and suddenly they were all dodging the animated metallic bodies as they charged at them. I sat there in shock that a professor could do such a thing. Weren't they supposed to teach us how to be good witches and vampires? Weren't they supposed to protect us from stuff like this? How could he be doing this to us? How could he have been hired with such hatred in his heart?

My heart was beating a thousand miles a minute, but my feet wouldn't move. My body wouldn't move. A chair rose in the air in front of me and then I was pulled from my seat, slammed in the side and landed on the floor as the chair crashed into the spot I'd just left. I looked up at James who had tackled me.

"You okay?" he asked softly.

I nodded.

James helped me to stand. He pulled me to my feet right as a desk came flying in our direction.

"James!" I screamed, terrified that it was about to hit us.

Moving faster than I ever thought possible, James spun us out of the way.

The desk slammed into the wall on our right and then rose up again, swirling in the air above our heads with most of the other chairs, tables and desks. I screamed again as a chair flew out of the swirl straight at a kid named Jarrod. He was a Strigoi, but he wasn't one of Cory and James friends, so I didn't know him well. He dodged the chair just in time and the chair smacked into the floor before lifting back up into the swirl.

My eyes flew to the professor who stood at the front of class. He was chanting, his eyes taking on an eerie black hue that covered the entire pupil. He was directing the mass of furniture in the air. Chanting to aim the pieces at the numerous vampires around the room and me.

James moved from my side and Professor Chalcedony's all black eyes tracked him. He dodged as the professor aimed a large table at him, but he wasn't fast enough or the table was too big to dodge entirely.

It clipped his shoulder and sent James down to the ground.

I watched Professor Chalcedony grin manically as James fell.

As James began to get up, I decided I couldn't take it any longer. I had to do something, before someone was seriously injured. I began pulling in energy as Professor Ubel had taught me. It took a moment for me to build it up enough. I watched James frantically dodge to his right again as a desk slammed into the wall where he'd been standing moments before.

The other witches in class sat, as if under a trance at their non-moving desks. They were not moving either, and their jaws hung open in disbelief. I couldn't believe none of them had stepped in to help counter this, but then again, none of them shared the magic I did, so they probably wouldn't be very effective. Still, they could do something to help.

Giving them a look of disgust, I threw out some counter-magic, just as another desk flew through the air toward James. My spell hit it and it went flying in the opposite direction, hitting the whiteboard at the front of the class and cracking it. *Oops,* I thought, *I hope that can be fixed.*

Professor Chalcedony's eyes turned on me, and suddenly all of the animated furniture shifted direction. To *my* direction. Panicked, I sent out spell after spell, slamming them into the desks, and chairs and tables as I'd done to the spiders in the courtyard. I looked back up into Professor Chalcedony's face, and it dawned on me. The automatons were his! He was the one behind the attacks.

"James!" I shouted, calling his attention. "The spiders and bats! He controls them!"

I glanced over at James as I sent another counter-magic spell toward another chair. James' face contorted and he became full on vampire, his fangs coming out and his eyes taking on a blood ring, even though it was still daylight out and his powers were muted.

"What!" he hissed, and his eyes flashed to the professor.

"I think he's also the one who enchanted my phone!" I accused loudly, staring at the professor.

Professor Chalcedony took a step back, his eyes returning to their regular crazed look. The animated furniture stopped swirling.

"Look out!" I shouted.

Within milliseconds, the Strigoi all darted toward the witches on the left side of the room, pulling them from their chairs and covered them against the wall, protecting them from what was about to happen.

The furniture dropped, slamming into the floor in

the middle of the room as the professor stopped chanting. He looked at us with such hatred as he turned and fled the room.

"We have to stop him before he gets too far!" I called, but James was already out the door.

"James!" Bethany shouted, looking over at me and then at the professor. "The spiders and bats! He controls them!"

Bethany glanced back over to me as she sent another counter-magic spell toward another chair. She was getting really good at those short blast spells, I thought for a moment, taking in her words.

My face contorted and I felt my fangs come out and my eye sight shifted to predator. I glanced at the window wonder how it was even possible for me to be vamping out like this in the morning light, but when I looked outside, the day seemed to be changing rather quickly. My powers seemed to be filling me and I wasn't sure what to make of it, but I put it out of my head to exam later when we weren't under attack.

"What!" I hissed, flicking my eyes to Professor Chalcedony.

"I think he's also the one who enchanted my phone!" Bethany accused. She said it loudly, as she stared daggers at the professor.

Professor Chalcedony took a step back, and I noticed the black shell leave his eyes. He still looked like the zealot that he normally portrayed in class, but somehow, more insane.

My eyes flicked up to the ceiling to the animated furniture as it stopped swirling.

"Look out!" Bethany shouted.

Within milliseconds, I sent out the message that we needed to protect the witches. The rest of the Strigoi in the room all darted across the center of the classroom and pulled the witches from their chairs, covering them physically from the furniture that was falling to the floor, protecting them since we could take more damage than they could.

The furniture plummeted in the next second, slamming into the floor in the middle of the room, bouncing and sliding to where the witches had just been moments before.

Professor Chalcedony was no longer chanting. I stared at him, wondering what he was going to do, but he seemed to be a little panicked as he stared at me with disgust. His eyes flicked to the door and I knew he was going to run. In the next second, Professor Chalcedony took off out of the room with me close on his heels.

I heard Bethany call, "We have to stop him before he gets too far!" but I was already out the door and about ten paces behind him.

Professor Chalcedony looked over his shoulder and saw me racing toward him. He turned back to face forward and ran faster. And then a potted plant flew at my head and I had to duck. It hit the center of my back and knocked me to the ground and the Professor gained some ground.

Another pot came flying in my direction, but it missed me as I slid across the floor and hit the wall. Standing, I could feel more power building and I glanced at the window, seeing the sky darkening more, as if it was nearing twilight instead of noon. I had no idea how that was happening, but I was thankful to whoever was causing it. I pushed from the wall and took off after the professor again. He'd gotten farther ahead as I'd taken that moment to stare outside in wonder.

"Damn," I muttered and then I heard Bethany behind me and I knew I wouldn't be able to go at full speed if she was going to try to keep up. There was no way she would be able to stay with me unless I went back for her.

Right then, a loud round of howls sounded from outside and it brought me to a stop for a moment as I paused to look out and see what was causing the noise. Shock hit me as I took in the large pack of chupacabras amassing near the treeline. Shaking my head, I took off again. I'd have to contemplate the meaning of the chupacabras later. I needed to catch Professor Chalcedony before he had a chance to call on his automatons to invade the school. I didn't want to put anymore students' lives at risk than I had to.

"James!" I heard Bethany shout from somewhere behind me.

"Here!" I called out, hoping she'd be able to pick up my location. I tried to slow my pace just a little as I headed for the stairs.

"James!" Bethany shouted again, she sounded breathless and near collapse. "I can't keep up!"

Frowning, I knew I didn't want to fight Professor Chalcedony on my own especially since even though I could feel my powers returning to me, I wasn't at full potential yet, but Bethany had her magic, even if she only used defensive magic, it was better than none at all.

I spun on my heel and raced back to her, picking

her up and swung her onto my back. "Hang on tight!" I urged, desperately trying to beat back the fear I felt at having her along with me, but I knew she was safest by my side where I could keep an eye on her.

"G o!" Micah, another Strigoi called to me across the room, his blue eyes ringed with red darting to the door. "We'll make sure they are all well."

I nodded. "Send someone to tell Professor Singh and Professor Ubel!" I called as I hurried out the door behind James.

I saw him rounding a corner, ducking as potted plants flew at him. One of the pots hit him and he went to the ground under it, but quickly got to his feet, so I didn't worry too much. I jumped over the spilled plants, racing after him. He was still fast, even though he didn't have all of his powers in the daylight.

With a glance at the window, I noticed that it was getting rather dark out, but I didn't understand why.

It wasn't evening, it was only about ten in the morning. I paused my steps and looked out the window up at the sky, and then across the lawn. Sure enough, the sun was at the horizon, setting.

"How in the world is this possible?" I thought as a round of howls sounded through the air. "What the heck is that?" I asked, staring out the windows onto the campus grounds.

"I don't know, but this is some freaking stuff going on!" a passing witch said as they rushed past me. "I'm going to my room, forget classes, girl!"

I shook my head. This wasn't something I could ignore. I stared out into the growing darkness and finally noticed a mass of shadows moving closer to the building. My heart began to race in my chest at the sight of them. And then suddenly the moon, full and bright as day rose in the sky, illuminating the shadows and I saw what they were.

Chupacabras.

A whole huge pack of them.

I counted the ones I could see, seeing ten of them and I shivered knowing there were probably more. My eyes darted back down the hall and I realized that I'd lost track of James and Professor Chalcedony.

"Crap!" I swore and took off down the hall, following the mess of destroyed plants and pottery.

I raced over the obstacles, hoping I was catching

up to them. However, with the day suddenly becoming night, I knew it would affect the vampires. More importantly, it would affect James. He'd be stronger, faster now. And I might not be able to catch up.

"James!" I called as I ran, dodging students moving in the opposite direction.

"Here!" His voice sounded not too far away, maybe at the end of the next hallway.

I turned a corner and saw him sprinting toward the stairs. "James!" I called again. "I can't keep up!"

Within a second, he was by my side, picking me up and swinging me onto his back. "Hang on tight!" he shouted as he took off again.

I clung to him as he swiftly jumped down the stairs and took off through the main hallway. I glanced up and saw Professor Chalcedony. We were catching up to him. "Look out!" I screamed as a couch flew at us.

I needn't have worried though. James punched the couch and it flew to the left of us, slammed to the ground and slid ten feet. Professor Chalcedony didn't stop with the couch. Furniture continued to fly at our heads, but James battled on, batting the overstuffed furnishings out of our way.

I giggled as I looked behind us at the clouds of cotton in the air. I knew it wasn't really the time for levity, but I couldn't help it. The main hall looked like a giant pillow fight had gone on. "Oh boy, I hope we don't get in trouble for this mess!" I commented as James sprinted on. I squeezed my legs around James' waist and looked forward again, enjoying the chase. I was ready to kick some ass and I knew exactly whose ass I was ready to kick!

CHAPTER 30
BETHANY

"H e's leaving the main building!" I called and pointed toward the doors as I clung to his fast moving body like a spider monkey.

"I see him," James commented, his voice sounding normal.

I couldn't believe he could run with me on his back like this and not be even a little out of breath. I would have been dead tired on the floor four hallways back if it were me carrying him. His powers must have finally grown to full strength. "Can we catch him?" I asked.

"I think so." James kept moving us farther down the hall. "Do you want to stay in the building or go with me out there?" He sounded hesitant, as though he didn't really want to leave me behind, but would if I wanted him to.

I frowned, not that he could see it. "Of course I'm going with you! I'm not letting you go after him all by yourself!" I declared. "Why would you even think otherwise?"

"The wards. You're safer in here."

"I'm safer with you!" I fired back. "No hesitation, just go."

"Okay." James nodded and slammed into the doors seconds later, not stopping his momentum, he continued out into the side yard of the school. "Look, he's headed toward that old laboratory!" James pointed across the field where we played soccer to the only rundown abandoned building on the campus.

I heard the pack of Chupacabra again, howling on the other side of the school.

"Is that what I think it is?" he asked as we started across the field.

"The Chupacabra. Yes."

"But…" James stopped speaking for a moment, "I saw them, there are more than the one who helped you before."

"I know. I counted at least ten, but I know there are more than that. It's a whole pack of them. I think the Ancient is behind all this help."

"The full moon and night you mean?" James asked.

I nodded and then realized with me on his back he wouldn't know it. "Yeah, I think this Ancient being made it full night for you. To make you stronger. And sent the Chupacabra to help."

James nodded. "Could be. I hope you're right anyway."

Just as we reached the far side of the field, Professor Ubel appeared on the north side of the field, striding toward us at an angle.

James stopped, but kept his eyes on the building we'd seen Professor Chalcedony disappear into. "Keep an eye on the old lab, sweetheart, if that asshole leaves the building we'll be on the chase again."

"Okay," I said softly.

"Professor Ubel, did you see Professor Chalcedony go in there?" James asked, nodding toward the building, but it really sounded more like a demand.

Professor Ubel stopped in front of us, drawing himself up to his full height and looked down at us in a haughty manner. "What business is it of yours where Professor Chalcedony goes? And what are the two of you doing out of class? Did you have something to do with all of this?" He waved his hand in the air.

I laid a hand on James' arm, calming him. I gave Professor Ubel a smile. "I'm sorry, Professor Ubel, but while we were in our History of the Magical World class, Professor Chalcedony attacked us. He animated all of the desks and chairs and set them to attack the Strigoi members of our class. I accused him of being the one to send the spiders and bats after me, and enchanting my phone. When I did, he fled the room and we've been chasing after him ever since."

"And what of all this?" Professor Ubel asked again as he waved his hand through the air. "Turning day into night? You expect me to believe he did that too?" He looked at us with an incredulous look.

"No, Professor. We aren't sure why the day turned to night," I replied, keeping my mouth shut about the Ancient we assumed was helping us.

"And where is that blessed howling coming from?" he continued, as he peered out into the night.

"Not sure, Professor," James murmured. "But we need to catch Professor Chalcedony and take him to Professor Singh."

"Why would you take him to Professor Singh?" he asked frowning. "Surely *if* he attacked students, you should take him to Professor Zin and have her call in the board."

I got the eerie feeling that he didn't believe us. "Professor Ubel—"

Professor Ubel looked at me and smiled. "What is it, my dear girl?"

"Professor, will you help us? He might listen to you and go with you," I suggested, hoping he would agree.

He gave us considering looks and then sighed as if we'd just asked him to save the world single handedly. "I suppose I had better at least go with you, just in case you are correct. We wouldn't want the two of you getting into any more tr—"

"Shadow spiders!" I screamed as a flood of the animated creatures of various sizes spilled out of the building we'd seen Professor Chalcedony disappear into.

They were coming from every possible opening, doors, windows, and then through the roof... bats! They were everywhere, filling the sky above our heads. Way too many for us to battle all on our own and they were all coming right toward us.

CHAPTER 31
BETHANY

Professor Ubel turned around and faced the shadow spiders. "Hmmm. I suppose you may be correct about Professor Chalcedony. Get back!" he commented urging us to move backwards across the field where we'd come from. "Bethany, my dear girl, pull in your energy. Now!"

I looked over at James and he nodded.

"You okay?" I asked as I watched him move to a crouch.

"I'm fine," he said through his fangs. "Do as Professor Ubel suggested, pull in your energy, this is going to be a battle."

I nodded, a shiver going through me at the masses of spiders moving toward us, the larger ones climbing over the smaller ones so they'd reach us first. My eyes flicked up to the sky and took in the bats swarming above us. Swallowing hard, I began to draw in energy. My hands began to glow and I formed energy balls and began launching them at the spiders and bats when they swooped down toward us. It didn't matter a whole lot. Those that I blasted were just replaced with another three it seemed.

I glanced at Professor Ubel and noticed he was using a different type of counter magic than my own. His seemed to be a softer version, but it seemed just as effective as the spiders he targeted crumpled and died as he hit them.

James grappled with a large spider, breaking its legs and pounding his fist through its head. I watched as he tossed it aside and then moved on to another.

I continued to throw spells, but the spiders and bats seemed to be gaining in strength, taking me more energy to put them down. "They're getting stronger!" I called. "How is that possible?" I asked, not really expecting an answer.

"I don't know!" James shouted back as he jumped in the air, grabbing the wings of a bat and ripping them off the creature.

"The smaller ones were easier to take out, but the bigger they get, the harder they are to counter!" I called as I formed a larger ball of energy and blasted a medium sized spider as it jumped at me.

"Fall back!" Professor Ubel called moving backwards toward me.

We did as he suggested and moved backwards over the hill and then past the copse of trees. We both continued to send magic at the automatons, but they were starting to overwhelm us.

"What's this?" a piercing voice shouted from behind the spiders. "Are my shadow pets winning against the famed prodigy, Bethany Welch?"

Professor Chalcedony moved between the large spiders, stroking their legs as he glanced up at his bats. He turned his gaze on us grinned manically as he said, "Tell me, Strigoi, do you regret what your species have done to us witches?" He looked at James, his eyes were black again and sparkled darkly in the moonlight.

"We did nothing to the witches that they didn't do to us first!" James shouted and took out another medium spider.

"Aw, look what you did to my little friend. No worries though, there are so many more to take his place. And his energy isn't wasted, is it?" he gloated and looked up at the largest spiders and bats, and then to Professor Ubel. "No sir, that energy just goes right to my large pets here."

I looked at him in horror. No wonder they were getting stronger! How in the world were we supposed to fight them? And where was Professor Singh and the Dusk Knights? Shouldn't they be here helping with this? I looked over my shoulder, hoping to see them heading our way, but there was nothing but darkness behind us.

"Looking for your saviors, Bethany?" Professor Chalcedony chuckled. "The Dusk Knights are..." He laughed again. "Otherwise occupied with more of my special pets."

My jaw clenched and I drew in as much energy as I could. While Professor Chalcedony had been talking, his shadow spiders and bats had stopped, well, sort of. They were still animated, but the spiders stood where they were, clicking their pinchers and making that loud tick, tick, tick sound as the bats hovered in place making the same tick- tick- tick as the spiders. I used the pause in the battle to build a large enough mass of energy that it might take out one of the giant spiders.

"Why are you doing this?" I asked, attempting to stall him. "Why are you attacking me?"

"Why? Why you ask? You petulant, vile girl who befriends the disgusting vampires who destroy our race? You ask me *why*?" Professor Chalcedony raged at me. He threw his head back and laughed. He sounded like a demented maniac. Once he finished, he stopped abruptly and stared at me. "Rip her to shreds!"

James sped across the field and flung himself in front of me, blocking me from the spiders.

I pushed the massive ball of energy at the closest spider and it stuttered back into its brothers, knocking a few of them off their legs. It didn't take them long to raise back up and move forward again, their pinchers reaching toward us as the bats dove directly at me and James.

"Bethany!" James shouted. "Run!"

CHAPTER 32
BETHANY

anicked, I started backing away again. I didn't want to turn my back on the automatons and have them pounce on me. As I backed away I began to hear a series of howls and then something hit the back of my legs and I fell, landing on my butt, narrowly missing being a bat meal. The chupacabra pack had arrived. I covered my head with my arms and pulled myself into a ball as the pack raced around me toward the spiders and leaping into the air at the bats. All but one chupacabra who stood directly in front of me as if protecting me.

"What the hell?" James called as a chupacabra tore into the spider directly in front of him.

"James!" I called, peeking up and over the chupacabra in front of me.

James raced to my side. "I'm here, where did they come from?"

I shook my head. "I don't know!" I watched as the chupacabra ripped into the automatons attacking us with gusto.

"Damn it, kill her!" Professor Chalcedony screamed at the automatons. "You stupid creatures! Go after her!" He stomped his feet and swore a litany of foul words.

We watched as the chupacabras began making headway with the spiders and bats, ripping legs, wings, and pinchers away, as they crunched in their teeth and shredded with their claws. Professor Ubel still seemed to be battling as many of the creatures as he could, the bats seemed to leave him alone as he continued taking out little and medium sized automatons.

The chupacabra in front of me began backing up. It looked over its shoulder at me and barked, urging me to move back more. James and I did as it directed, backing up slowly. Once we were a fair distance away, the chupacabra looked at me again and barked twice. Somehow, I knew what it wanted me to do. I nodded and began drawing in energy. Once I had enough, I created a massive shield around James and me.

The chupacabra nodded its massive head and

then took off toward the spiders and bats, diving into the fight.

"How did you know that was what it wanted?" James asked, incredulous.

"I—" I had no idea how I knew. I looked at him blankly and shrugged. "I don't know. It was just, like this urgent feeling. Like it said '*Protection. Now.*' And I understood it."

We watched the battle, with Professor Chalcedony becoming even more and more unhinged. The bats and spiders were able to take out a few of the chupacabras, tossing them through the air with their giant pinchers and talons. The chupacabras' bodies mummified and then turned to ash. With each of their deaths I felt this piercing of my heart. These creatures were my protectors and I didn't want to see them die.

The main chupacabra, the one who'd first engaged with me, swung his head toward me, his eyes staring directly in mine as if he could feel my hurt for them. He barked three times and somehow I knew that they were at peace. That this was exactly the purpose they were created to defend against.

There were still a great many chupacabras in the fight, more than the ten I'd thought I counted. It was hard to say for sure, but it seemed as if there were at least fifty now in the fight. It was hard to tell with the hundreds of spiders and bats everywhere, both dead and alive. Their bodies, unlike the chupacabras didn't mummify and turn to ash. They just shriveled up into empty carcasses. It was going to leave a massive mess once all of this was over.

"Stop engaging the dogs! Go after the girl, you stupid automatons! Obey your master! Go after the girl, you idiotic beings!" Professor Chalcedony ranted at the bats and spiders.

As we watched several of the large spiders stopped their movement forward toward us. Their pinchers clicked loudly and fast. Tick-tick-tick-tick! The bats stopped in mid-air, switching directions and moving back toward Professor Chalcedony. As if they were all one being, the spiders turned toward the center where Professor Chalcedony stood.

"What are you doing?" Professor Chalcedony looked at the bats and spiders with horror. "I created you! Do what you're told! Go after the girl!" He began backing away, panic clear on his face and in his voice.

The spiders moved closer to him and the bats hovered directly over his head. The chupacabras began to back away from them, moving out of their way as they formed a circle around Professor Chalcedony, allowing the automatons to do what they intended now that the threat was no longer focused on Bethany and James.

"What— what are you doing? What's going on? Why are you— No! Get away! No! Professor Ubel! Help me!" Professor Chalcedony screamed in terror. "No! Stop!" He batted at the pinchers reaching for him. The bat wings hit him in the head as the talons reached for him.

James pulled my face into his shoulder so I couldn't see. "Don't look, beautiful," he whispered.

"Okay," I commented. But I could still hear everything.

"No! Stop! Ubel! Help me! You said— Aaaaaaaaah!"

Crunch!

Crush!

Crick!

Spurt!

I cringed with every sound that came from the spiders and bats ripping Professor Chalcedony to pieces. And although I hadn't actually seen anything, I had a very vivid imagination. I'd be having nightmares about this day for years to come I was sure. After a few minutes everything went quiet. "Is it over?" I asked softly.

James let me lift my head up, but he kept me facing him. "It is, but don't look."

"Okay," I breathed. "Are the chupacabra all alright?"

James nodded. "Yes, it seems so, once the bats and spiders... well most of them left. Just the one still here now."

"Can I see?"

"Not yet. Professor Ubel is driving the rest of the spiders back with some of the Dusk Knights who've finally shown up."

I looked up at his face. "They aren't going after the chupacabra are they?" I was worried that they would be fearful of my protectors.

James smiled. "No, just the spiders and bats."

"Good." I nodded.

"Okay, it's mostly clear now."

I turned to see the chupacabra about three feet

away. It was facing me, as if waiting for me to look at it. When I met its eyes, it seemed to be asking if I was alright.

"I'm fine now, thank you," I said to it.

The chupacabra lowered its head in a nod, gave me a bark and then took off after its pack.

I turned to look over the scene. There were tons of spider and bat bodies everywhere. The Dusk Knights seemed to be gathering them and putting them in a pile. I felt overwhelmed at the scene and was suddenly exhausted.

"Miss Welch, Mr. Barret, I think it would be best if you returned to your dorms, now. We'll handle this mess," Professor Ubel said wearily, wiping sweat from his forehead.

"Yes, sir." James nodded as he hugged me to him.

"Thank you, Professor."

"I'm just glad I was here to help, my dear girl. Go now. Rest. You're going to need it."

I don't know why, but his words made a shiver of terror race up my spine.

❦

WHEN WE REACHED MY DORM ROOM, JAMES KISSED my forehead. "Are you going to be okay for a while?"

I gripped his shirt. "You've got to go to the nurse, don't you," I said, my voice small and quiet.

"If I could stay here with you, I would. But I have to eat or..."

I nodded. "I know." I sighed and hugged him to me again. "I'll be okay."

James lifted my chin and kissed me. "You will." He smiled. "You've got a great many protectors out there. Not just me."

I smiled too. "I know. I don't know why. I'm not that special."

"You're wrong about that, beautiful. You are the most special being on the planet to me."

I blushed at his words and met his eyes. "I'm glad you were with me out there."

"As I recall, you insisted I bring you with me," I grinned at her and then became more serious. "I will always be there with you," I promised. "No matter what you face, I will be by your side."

I took a deep breath and smiled again, his words warming my heart. "You'd better go before I decide not to let you leave."

James grinned, he kissed my cheek and then sped off down the hallway.

With a sigh, I pushed into my room and pulled my phone from my back pocket. We had to keep it on silent during school hours, but I normally had it on vibrate.

Looking at it, I realized I had turned it off completely. I hit the button to see that I had about twelve missed calls from my mom. That made me panic. Was everything okay at home? Had the Shadow Society decided since they couldn't get to me, they'd go after my family?

With my heart racing, I clicked voicemail and then listened to the messages. They all said mostly the same thing and I breathed a sigh of relief.

"Bethany, why are you not answering your phone? Are you screening your calls?"

"Bethany, this is your mother. Call me."

"It's me again. Your mother. Call me."

"Why do you even have a phone if you aren't going to answer?"

I hit erase after each one and then hit the call Mom button.

She answered after the first ring. "Bethany! Where have you been?"

"Hi, Mom. Sorry, I was in class, it is a school day, you know. We have to keep our phones off. Everything alright at home?" I asked, curious since she didn't usually call like this unless it was Thanksgiving or Christmas. Of course, now that I thought about it, she hadn't called this past Thanksgiving, but Dad had. I frowned recalling Mom had gone to her sisters for the occasion, but Dad hadn't wanted to go because they'd been planning a massive shopping trip for Black Friday.

"Can a mother not just want to hear from her daughter?" She sounded offended that I was questioning her about it.

I sighed and rolled my eyes. "Of course, you can, but was there something, I don't know, urgent or something? You called twelve times."

"Well, no, not really. I was just wondering how your classes were going, sweetie."

"Um, well, this has been an interesting semester. We've got finals next week, then a week off. Christmas you know. Did you want me to come home for it?"

"Oh, no, that's not necessary. You remember me suggesting last July that we take a cruise?"

I vaguely recalled a conversation about summer trips and Mom mentioning a cruise. "Sort of, did you find one for us to go on next summer?" I asked confused about why she would call me now about our summer trip.

"No, no, sorry. It's not about summer. Your father and I have decided we are taking a cruise over Christmas and New Year's. A romantic trip to rekindle the romance with a Caribbean trip. Won't that be fun?"

"Uh, yeah, sure Mom. You and Dad have a good time."

"Well, since we won't see you, I'm sending your gifts in the mail. Was there anything special you were wanting?" she asked.

"No. Not really." I flopped back on my bed, draping my other arm across my eyes and held back the sigh I felt building.

"Hmmm. Well what else has been going on? Have you met any other nice boys?"

"No, Mom. I'm still dating James," I told her, knowing she was fishing for the information.

She sighed. "You know I worry about that, with him being... well..."

"I know, Mom. However, there is nothing to worry about with James. I promise. Dad said he talked to you about him when I talked to him on Thanksgiving while you were at Aunt Susan's. He said you agreed to allow me to keep seeing him." I stood up and walked over to my desk, flipping through my History of the Magical World book, but not really looking at the pages.

"I know. I did tell him I wouldn't put up a fuss if he wouldn't put up a fuss about... Nevermind. It's just, I still worry about you, sweetie. I'm your mother, it's my job to worry."

I knew she'd been referring to the Black Friday

shopping she had been planning at the time. Dad had used it as leverage for me. "Well, you shouldn't worry about James. He would never hurt me."

You should worry about hateful professors who are trying to kill me, I thought.

"And you're sure you are alright?" she asked hesitantly, not letting it drop. "It's just... I've had the strangest feeling all day that something was terribly wrong with you."

I smiled. Mom had always had great intuition. It made me wonder if there was something to that whole erasing my family from witch history thing we had considered last year.

"I promise I am perfectly fine, Mom. Nothing to worry about here. Unless that feeling involves me flunking my History of the Magical World final, because that is a real possibility if I don't get to studying."

"Oh, then go, darling, I won't keep you."

I smiled. "Bye, Mom. Love you."

"Bye, sweetie, love you too!"

I hung up and fell face first on my bed. I was asleep in seconds.

CHAPTER 34

JAMES

When I left Bethany at her dorm, I hurried to the nursing station, completely famished. I felt as though I was seconds from tearing into someone's neck. When I reached the station, and the nurse caught sight of me, she directed me into a cubicle and grabbed a bag of blood from the emergency stash and handed it to me with a straw.

I gulped the bag down and finally the feeling of desperation subsided. Had I waited any longer, I probably would have fallen sick. I glanced up into the nurse's face and she frowned at me.

"Now what in the blazes have you been up to that you got like that?" she asked, tapping her foot on the floor.

I wiped my mouth with the back of my hand.

"There was a battle, with spiders and bats. Not real ones, but automatons. Professor Chalcedony... he ... well he's the one behind them."

"And you had to be the one to take him on?" She arched her brow at me.

"He started it," I muttered.

"Hmmm." She hissed as she pulled out her stethoscope and pushed me back in the chair. "Your heartbeat is still fast. I'll get you another bag. Stay here." She frowned at me as if I would leave.

I nodded.

She returned about fifteen minutes later with the bag, a new straw and the clipboard. She handed it to me first. "Sign in. Put the time at four ten."

"Yes, ma'am." I did as she said and handed it back to her.

She made a few notes and then set the board aside. She unlocked the cabinet above her head and made a few more notes on the door and then pulled out the scalpel. Picking up the blood bag, she sliced into the thick bag and then she stabbed the straw in and handed it to me. "Drink," she ordered before turning back to the cabinet and replacing the scalpel and locking it.

I took the bag and drank the entire thing in about three minutes. When I finished, she disposed of it and the straw in their proper receptacles and then listened to my chest again. "Well?"

"Better." She sighed. "Still, I'd feel better if you had a bit more. I'll go get a small bag."

"I don't think—"

"You will have another small bag and you will not argue about it. Do you understand me, young man?" she hissed, her fangs showing and her hands on her hips.

I bit back a smile. "Yes, ma'am."

With a nod, she left the room again. She returned within five minutes this time. "Here."

I took the already prepped bag and drank it down. I felt extremely full and I could feel every cut and abrasion I'd received in the battle begin to heal more quickly. As I handed it back to her, I said, "Thank you."

"Now, you come see me before you go engaging in anymore of these battles. Especially ones with professors."

"Yes, ma'am." I grinned.

"What happened to that professor? He's that nasty one isn't he? The one always berating us?"

"He berated the staff too?" I questioned, surprised. "How the heck did he even get hired?"

"I have no idea. As far as we are aware, the board

sent him. Anyway, how did he fair in this battle of yours?"

"He died."

The nurse blinked. "You killed him?" she asked in surprise.

"No, the spiders and bats did. It wasn't pretty."

"Huh. Good. He probably deserved worse."

I nodded. "Yes, my thoughts exactly."

"You're free to go. Don't go stirring up any more trouble, alright?"

"I'll do my best not to."

Leaving the nursing station, I headed back to the dorms. While I felt full and mostly healed, I knew I needed to rest to get back to one hundred percent.

"What the heck happened to you? Rumor is Professor Chalcedony completely freaked out in class and you went after him."

I glanced at Cory and dropped down on the bed. "Long story."

"You got somewhere to be?"

I huffed out a laugh. "No. Not right now. Where to even start?"

"The beginning, man, always start at the beginning," Cory suggested getting comfortable on his own bed. "Spill it."

So I did.

CHAPTER 35

BETHANY

I woke early the next morning and headed to the cafeteria after taking a shower and dressing for the day. I picked up a platter of pancakes and ate them on my own. I could feel all the stares from everyone around the room as if they crawled over my skin. I finished my food quickly and downed my glass of milk. When I finished, I headed off to find Professor Singh.

I wanted to know if she'd found anything out about why Professor Chalcedony attacked me. I made my way to her lab and knocked on the door.

"Come in."

"Good morning, Professor Singh."

"Ah, Miss Welch. I have been wondering when I would see you."

"You have?"

She smiled. "I imagined after that battle yesterday that I would be your first stop. I was surprised I didn't find you in my office after it all happened."

I laughed. "Well, I knew the Dusk Knights were cleaning up, so I assumed you were out there too." I paused as I recalled Professor Chalcedony saying she and the Dusk Knights were otherwise engaged. "You all are okay too, aren't you? Professor Chalcedony claimed you were busy and couldn't help us with the spiders and bats, but Professor Ubel was there and he helped us."

At the mention of Professor Ubel she frowned for a moment and then shook her head. "We are fine, Miss Welch. I imagine Professor Chalcedony was alluding to the second Chinese Hopper he set off in town. We were able to contain it before too many civilians were injured."

"Another one?" I asked incredulous.

"Yes, I've sent some Knights off to check the clan. Both were from the same one in Boston. I am worried that Chalcedony killed them all and was holding their bodies preparing to set them off one at a time as needed."

"How horrible."

"Yes. So I imagine you are here to find out why he was focused on you?"

"Yes, Professor," I agreed.

Professor Singh gestured to a seat at the lab table and I took it while she sat on a stool close by. "I am afraid I can only offer you my conjectures. He left nothing of his thoughts in the laboratory where he created those automatons. The building had been bespelled in such a way that made us look away from it while we made our rounds around campus. I should have suspected, being the warding teacher, but I fear he was better at it than we originally gave him credit for. As for what I believe... I believe he was mentally unstable and had a real fear of vampires. You, and your group of friends were a threat to everything he knew and believed. Which is why he targeted you."

"And you think that is all there is to it, Professor?" I asked, afraid to believe that everything was over. I had serious concerns about Professor Chalcedony's allegiance to the Shadow Society. Of course, I had no proof he was a member, but my intuition told me I was correct.

"I certainly hope so, Bethany. For your sake." She shook her head. "You've been put through more than any one student should ever have to go through."

I smiled. "Thank you, Professor."

"I'm keeping the wards up on your room, but you should be able to go about outside now without being attacked. The Dusk Knights and I were able to disable and destroy the remaining automatons. There weren't any Formless Ones possessing any of them. Just be careful and keep your eyes open." She patted my arm. "Oh, I've been meaning to ask... the chupacabras... where did they come from?"

"I have no idea, Professor. One protected me before, but this time there was a whole pack of them. I did see them come from the woods if that helps?"

"You seemed to be engaging with one of them, can you tell me how?"

I nodded. "Well, I'm not sure. It barked at me, and it was as if I could understand what it wanted. More of a feeling rather than actual words, kind of like telepathy, but more with feelings than words or images."

Professor Singh nodded. "Well, you are one lucky young witch to have them looking after you."

"I know, Professor." I smiled.

"You had best be on your way, I imagine you have semester finals to study for."

"I do." I started to stand. "Professor?"

"Yes, Miss Welch?"

"Um, who is going to take over Professor Chalcedony's class? History of the Magical World?"

"Professor Corbett has agreed to take on the class. Much to the relief of the Strigoi in his classes. I imagine you all will have to redo the semester, seeing as everything I've heard Professor Chalcedony taught was a bunch of rubbish."

"Yes ma'am, it really was very biased against the vampires," I acknowledged her information. "So there won't be an exam?"

"I doubt it, my dear. Though I'll leave that up to Professor Corbett to discuss with you all tomorrow."

"Thank you, Professor."

With a relieved smiled I headed down to the vampire dorms to give James the news.

CHAPTER 36

BETHANY

"**H**ave you already heard?" I asked as James opened the door and smiled at me.

"Hmmm, that depends on what we're talking about." He grinned and pulled me into his arms. Leaning down he brushed a kiss across my lips. "Are we talking about how much I love you? Or how much you love me? Because I would willingly hear that again." His eyes twinkled at me and his grin deepened.

I giggled. "Well, I definitely do love you. A lot. But that isn't what I was talking about." I smiled at him as I moved from his embrace and gripping his hand tugged him over to his bed. I pulled him down with me and then after he sat, threw my legs over his and snuggled into his side.

"Then what are you talking about, beautiful?"

"History of the Magical World."

"Ugh. That class." James frowned. "At least no more Chalcedony and his rhetoric. I wonder who's gonna teach now."

"That is what I was asking you about." I grinned at him. "Professor Corbett is going to teach and..." I drew the word out and then kissed his lips, "Professor Singh says he probably won't give us a mid-term exam!"

"Thank god. I was dreading having to study for it." He chuckled. "So, since it appears we now have one less class to study for, and considering you are now free to go out into the world, would you like to go into town?"

My thoughts brightened even more and I looked up at him. "Yes! Oh, can we go to China Star and then get ice cream and then maybe check out that comic book store of yours?"

James laughed. "Sure." He moved my legs off of his, and then standing pulled me up after him. "Do you need to change or anything first?"

I looked down at my jeans and pink sweater. "Do I not look okay?" I frowned at him.

"You look wonderful to me, but I know girls like to primp before dates, so..."

I rolled my eyes. "I do not primp. When have I ever?" I challenged.

He took a breath, and then shut his mouth and smiled at me. "Come on, you can borrow a coat from Jodie, I'm sure she has plenty, and then we'll go."

"Mmmmhmmm. Good dodge on that," I said with a laugh as I took his hand and we headed toward Jodie's room. I grabbed a coat and then we headed out of the building. I enjoyed being out in the fresh air without being attacked.

"Feel good?" James asked, squeezing my fingers.

"Definitely." I grinned back at him.

At the Chinese restaurant I ate my fill of sweet and sour chicken, lo mein and wonton soup. Then we headed over to the local ice cream shop and I had a two scoop bowl of lemon and double fudge ice cream. James stared at me as if I was crazy, but it was my favorite combination. Afterwards, we held hands as we walked to the comic book store. James showed me his favorites and then I picked up one for myself, the first of the *Border Town* series.

"You know I have that one, you could borrow it."

I smiled. "No, because if I like it, I'll want my own."

James just shook his head and smiled at me as he paid for it.

We ended the evening sitting at the top of the clock tower and I couldn't help but admire the way the moonlight glinted in his eyes right before he kissed me breathless.

CHAPTER 37
JAMES

I t was the start of Christmas break and I was relieved that not only had Bethany and I both passed our classes, we'd both made it through alive. We'd made plans for every day of the break we'd get since her parents were making her come home. I'd gotten special permission from Professor Zin to take Bethany for a weekend ski trip, not that she knew about it yet. I'd been a little worried about her parents saying no, especially since they'd worried about her dating someone like me, but Professor Zin had gained me their blessing when she made the call.

I planned to tell her about the trip on our date later. At the moment she was out shopping with Jodie, who was encouraging her to pick out clothing that would be appropriate for our skiing adventure. Jodie and Terrance were going as well, and we'd rented this great ski chalet in Aspen. I went to my closet and pulled out a small suitcase and prepared to pack. As I moved to my dresser, my eye landed on the book the Librarian had given me.

"Hmmm," I muttered as I looked at it. I'd been putting off returning it, because I'd been having some thoughts about the Librarian and I wasn't sure how to approach them about it. However I didn't want to hold off returning it until after the ski trip. Sighing, I decided I should get it out of the way now, before I packed.

I picked up the heavy book and steeling my nerves I headed out the door.

"Hey, what's up?" Cory asked as soon as I moved into the hall.

"Hey, not much, returning this to the Librarian, then coming back to pack before I go out with Bethany. Why?"

"I can't believe you got her parents' permission, man. Does Lindon know you won't be here for Christmas?" Cory arched a brow.

"Yeah man, of course."

"And he knows you're taking Bethany?"

"Yeah." I looked at him wondering where he was going with his questions. "Why?"

Cory shrugged. "You know what he's been like, hunting for the coven that sent the Formless One after Arrond. He's been a bit untrusting of witches recently."

"He doesn't have a problem with Bethany, Cory. Do you?" I asked, suddenly concerned.

"No." Cory looked down and then frowned at me.

"Then what is this?" I asked tilting my head at him.

He looked back up at me and I could see it in his eyes. He was *jealous*. He shrugged and looked away.

"Cors, you know I'll be back, right? It's just the weekend. You're still my best friend."

Cory sighed. "I know. Just I don't like change and with Bethany in your life…"

"You think I don't have time for you," I finished for him.

Cory shrugged again.

"Man, we gotta get you a girl."

Cory rolled his eyes. "That is the last thing I need. A girl changes everything."

I grinned. "Not the right one." I clapped him on the shoulder. "Listen, Cors, Bethany isn't taking me from you. We'll still hang out, still do stuff together. You're my brother, we're family."

Cory nodded. "I know. You're right. It's just that with you gone, Lindon wants me to come home for Christmas. He wants to drag me out looking for that coven."

I commiserated with him. "I get it. He dragged me all over the states during the summer. I think he just likes having company. Tell him you'll go, but you have to be back Monday because you're on the New Years' party committee."

Cory's face brightened. "Hey that might work."

"Good. I gotta get, or I'm gonna be late."

"See ya later." Cory waved as I headed down the hall toward the Library.

Lukas was of course lurking nearby and intercepted me. "Strigoi, what are you doing down here. Again."

"Just returning this to the Librarian, and I had some questions about it." I smiled.

Lukas frowned looking at the book. "Very well. Keep it short."

I nodded as he allowed me to pass into the Library. As I moved into the room, the Librarian appeared and welcomed me with a smile.

"Hello." I nodded.

The Librarian's smile widened and they gestured to the seats in front of a lit fireplace which made the area feel cozy.

I took the offered seat and then handed the book to the Librarian. "Thank you for this, I did not get the chance to read it all, but it was very helpful."

The Librarian grinned as if they knew I'd hardly read much of it.

I felt my pale cheeks heat. "I had a few questions."

The Librarian waited patiently for me to ask.

I didn't think they would actually answer, but I asked anyway. "Are you... the Ancient One?"

The Librarian smiled, but with a shrug, they didn't commit to answering.

I took a breath and tried again. "The chupacabras... did you send them?"

The Librarian continued to smile, but not really answering one way or another. They just stared at me, as if amused at me.

It was very frustrating and draining.

Sighing, I said, "Are the Formless Ones getting stronger?"

This time I received a full grin and a nod from the Librarian. They seemed pleased that I was now on this path of questions, so I continued.

"Is it the Shadow Society behind the attacks on Bethany?"

Nodding the Librarian stared at me, as if telling me to continue.

"Is the threat still here?" I asked softly.

They nodded again.

I drew in another breath. "Will the chupacabra continue to help protect Bethany?"

They smiled gently and nodded again.

"You are who I think you are, then."

They just smiled.

"Why are you helping her?" I asked, not because I didn't want the help in protecting her, but because I wanted to be sure that it was actual help.

The Librarian leaned forward and in a soft unearthly voice that was neither female, nor male, said, "Because some things are worth protecting."

Bethany's face came to my mind and I smiled in understanding. "Yes, yes they are," I agreed.

If you liked A Witch Against The Vampire, sign up here to find out when the next book, A Witch's Immunity, goes live!

ALSO BY SOPHIE CASTLE

Supernatural Academy

A Vampire Meets A Witch - Book 1

A Witch Against The Vampire - Book 2

A Witch's Immunity - Book 3

Printed in Great Britain
by Amazon

86694812R00194